D0875006

DAWN OF THE
HUNTER

THE OMEGA SERIES

One

AM I BITTER? YEAH, I'm bitter. Sometimes people ask me if I have lost my humanity. I tell them, not yet, but I'm working on it. I don't like humanity. I don't like people. There is the odd exception, but that's what they are – exceptions. That's why, when I came home to the States after ten years, I moved to the most remote, unpopulated State in the Union. Wyoming.

I like it here. It's a place where you can mind your own business and people—those that there are—let you get on with it, provided you keep your nose out of theirs. That suits me fine.

But the guy who rolled up in front of my workshop that morning in his Cadillac CTSV sedan was not an exception. He was not minding his own business and he sure as hell wasn't going to let me mind mine. He had it written all over his Aryan face, crew-cut platinum hair and his three thousand dollar Italian suit. I assumed his eyes were pale blue, but they were concealed behind very black Wayfarers.

You don't see a lot of Cadies in Boulder Flats, so when it rolled into my lot, off Boulder Flats Road, I had an idea where it had come from and who had sent it. And when the driver got out, I was sure.

"Lacklan Walker?"

"Who are you?"

He held out his hand. "Ben Smith. I work for your father."

I looked at his hand and then at his black shades. "What do you want?"

"Your father wants to see you."

"I don't want to see him."

He looked up at the sky. "That's what he said you'd say."

"He was right. Is there anything else?"

"He told me to tell you he was dying."

I walked away from him back into my shed, among the smell of engine oil, tools and old rags, where I felt at home. He followed me and stood silhouetted in the doorway, looking at the car I was working on. On the outside it looked like a matte black 1968 Mustang Fastback. That was the chassis it had. But what it had under the hood was something different.

"Sweet ride. Mustang '68?"

"Zombie 222, modified."

"I've spoken to the doctor myself. He has maybe six months, maybe less."

"What does he want from me?"

He sighed and removed his shades. His eyes were pale blue. For a moment he looked human. He moved to my workbench and rested his ass against it. "Do you want me to relay what he said, or do you want my opinion?"

I shrugged. "Neither, but go ahead, let's have both."

He stared at me, like he was trying to decide whether to send me to hell or not. "My opinion is that he has realized only now that he is not immortal, and that has focused his mind. He's realized that he has valued the wrong things in life, and now he doesn't know how to make amends. So he's reaching out to you, hoping it's not too late."

"They teach you that kind of shit on the CIA's Being a Human Being 1-0-1 course?"

"No, I learnt it myself, watching a lot of people die. You don't know me, Lacklan."

"So that's your opinion. What did he say?"

"He said he wants you to help Marni. She's in serious trouble."

I went cold inside. I walked around the car till I was only a couple of feet away from him. Outside the birds were singing in the early September sunlight. I could hear a dog barking across the fields, a diesel grinding down the road. But it felt unreal in the darkness of the barn, with this guy staring at me with his arms crossed, his black shades perched on his head.

"What kind of trouble?"

"You need to ask him that."

"Do you know?"

He shook his head. "And if I did, I wouldn't tell you." He shrugged and looked out at the sunshine. "But if she was in trouble with the law, or if it was financial..." He looked back and smiled at me. "He wouldn't call on you, would he? He'd call on your brother, Bob. So I'm guessing it's something that requires your special talents."

"Get out of my house, Mr. Smith. Tell my father I'll be there."

"He asked me to take you."

"I'll make my own way." I waited. He watched me. I said, "Leave."

He thought about it, then stood. "He's expecting you tonight, tomorrow at the latest." He waited for an answer, but I had nothing to say. He shrugged. "I'll see you in Boston, Lacklan."

He walked out into the sunshine and climbed into his Caddie. I stood at the door of my shed and watched him cruise out of sight down Boulder Flats Road. Something, some deep instinct, told me someday I'd have to kill him. And he wouldn't be easy to kill.

I spent half an hour putting the finishing touches to the modifications I'd made on the Zombie, extending its range to four hundred and fifty or five hundred miles, and its top speed to 200 MPH. Then I went inside. I made my way up to the attic and pulled out my kit bag. That's another modification of mine, based on the principle that you can never have too many weapons or too much ammunition. Most of the weapons I use are silent, with the exception of my Smith & Wesson 500, because surprise is the best advantage you'll ever have, but sometimes you need to blow down a wall.

Beside the Smith & Wesson cannon, the rest of the kit was a pair of field glasses, a take down orange osage bow, with twelve aluminum arrows that formed a removable, rigid frame for the bag, a 9 mm Sig Sauer P226 with six extended twenty round magazines, a Heckler and Koch G36 assault rifle with twelve thirty-round magazines and a Fairbairn-Sykes fighting knife with a brass, knurled grip. There was also spare 50 grain ammo for the Smith & Wesson, and a pair of night-vision goggles. On top of that, I had a dozen cakes of C4, wrapped in non-descript brown paper, a dozen M5 universal firing devices and a dozen remote detonators keyed to my cell.

I also had a second Sig 226 under my arm and a 232 in my boot. Like I said, you can never have too many weapons.

I slipped the Fairbairn-Sykes in my boot alongside the 232 and carried the kit bag down to the car. I put it in the trunk and went to lock up the house. I had a feeling I wouldn't be back for a while. On the way out I picked up four hundred Camel cigarettes and my brass Zippo.

I climbed in the Zombie and fired her up. There was no roar, no thunder, no sound at all. This machine delivers eight hundred bph, one thousand eight-hundred foot-pounds of torque straight to the back wheels, and will go 0-60 in just over one and a half seconds. And she is totally silent. Like I said, I favor the silent kill.

I took the 287 down to Rawlins, and then turned east on the I-80. It was going to be a thirty-two-hour drive, so I'd allow myself two hours sleep. I looked at my watch. It was eleven AM. I'd arrive around 9 PM the next day. I put the Eagles on the CarPlay, poked a Camel in my mouth and lit up.

I hadn't seen Marni for six years. It had been November. She'd come to London to see me for my birthday. Hers was in April. We were both twenty four. Young. We hadn't seen each other for almost five years—just once in the last ten. And before that we'd been each other's whole world. I asked myself how that happened. But I knew. I knew how it had happened.

I made it happen.

I could not let her be a part of what I had become. She was everything that was best in a human being. She was kind and decent and honorable, like her father; and like her father she had devoted her life to trying to make the world a better place in whatever way she could. Me? I was a killer, and I had devoted my life to becoming one of the best in my trade. I had risen with honor through the ranks of one of the most lethal regiments on Earth. The British SAS.

She had come to London to ask me to go back, to make a life with her in Boston. I had told her it could never happen. She had pleaded, I had died inside seeing her cry. But I had said no. And we had not seen each other or spoken to each other since. Now my father was using her, the way he used everybody and everything, to further his ends.

I drove throughout the day with a couple of short pit stops at roadside service stations to use the can and get a burger and a beer. I watched the sun go down in the big, flat, open spaces of Nebraska, and drove in deepening darkness, under the vast prairies of stars, through Iowa and into Illinois. There, at two AM, I pulled off the I-80 into the Hilltop Motel and slept in the parking lot for two hours. At four I moved on, silent and fast, along empty roads bathed in the dead light of dawn streetlamps, past Chicago on the shores of Lake Michigan. At eleven I stopped for a late breakfast outside Erie, and then moved on again, through upstate New York and into New Hampshire.

All the while my rage was mounting: against life for betraying all the hope and dreams that it breeds in you when you're a kid; and against my father, for the same reasons; for that, and for using his own mortality, and Marni, to manipulate me and seed fear in me.

The Zombie will do two hundred miles per hour, in total silence, without breaking a sweat. In my mounting rage I must have let my foot get heavy, because I arrived at Weston, just outside Boston, at seven PM, two hours ahead of schedule. If there were cops chasing me on the I-80 to give me a ticket, I wished them luck.

My father lived in a ten bedroom pile in the woods off Concord Road. I wound down the drive in the failing light, among the huge pines and ancient chestnut trees, and parked across from the fountain. The slam of the car door echoed like a shotgun among the autumn woodlands, and I heard crows flapping and cawing through the trees. I climbed the stairs between the two landscaped lawns and pulled the chain that made the bell ring in the servants' quarters. It was that kind of pile.

Kenny, the butler, who had served my father for the last thirty years, opened the door and looked pleased to see me.

"Mr. Walker, your father is in the library. He told us to expect you." He stood back to let me in. "Have you any bags?"

"It's in the trunk Kenny, but I'll deal with it myself." I gave him a look heavy with meaning and he almost smiled.

"Very good, sir."

He led the way to the library, opened the tall, walnut doors and announced me. My father didn't look up as I stepped into the room. He was sitting in his favorite, old chesterfield, with its scuffed, burgundy leather and chipped, wooden legs. The room was largely dark. There was one lamp on, but most of the light came from the log fire, and washed and flickered across his face. He had a blanket over his knees. I hadn't seen him in five years, but he had aged twenty in that time. When he spoke, he spoke to the flames.

"Come on in, Lacklan, help yourself to a drink. Grab a chair."

I wanted to tell him to go to hell, but something stopped me. Maybe it was the need to know what had happened to Marni, maybe it was the fact that he looked as though he was already there. Maybe it was both. Instead I walked to the salver on the map table by the leaded window, and poured myself a whiskey from the crystal decanter; a decanter that was probably worth more than a working man's monthly salary. I carried my drink to the wing chair opposite my father's and sat. Now he looked at me. I pulled out a Camel, poked it in my mouth and lit up. I blew out a stream of smoke and looked him in the eye.

"What do you want?"

"I need to tell you what happened, what I did...what I have done."

"I'm not interested."

"You have to be interested, Lacklan."

"Why?"

He looked haggard and raised a hand to pinch the bridge of his nose. His hand was shaking and his skin was gray.

"Because," he said, "Marni has been abducted."

Two

I FELT THE SKIN ON my face go cold. My heart gave a powerful jolt and for a moment the room seemed to rock. When I spoke, my voice was a rasp.

"What are you talking about?"

He nodded, like he was agreeing with something I had said. "The thing is, Lacklan, in order to explain, I need to go back, to tell you what happened, and what I did."

"Is this your fault? Did you make this happen?"

He nodded, and I could see tears in his eyes. "Yes. It's my fault. But if you are going to help Marni, you need to set that aside and listen to me."

We watched each other across the silence. Finally, I asked him, "What did you do?"

He reached out his hand. "Give me one of those damned cigarettes, will you?" I hesitated and his face flushed with sudden anger. "It's cancer of the liver! It will kill me long before any fucking cigarette does!"

I handed him the pack and the lighter. He lit up and smiled at the Zippo, squinting through the smoke. "Good American lighter. An institution."

He handed it back and I asked him again, "What did you do?"

He looked grave. "It's going to be a long night, Lacklan, and I am going to tell you things that you will probably not believe.

This isn't a sentimental need to unburden myself..." He paused, looking into the flames in the fire. "...though it's true enough I do want to confess to what I have done. But more important, I have to tell you all of this so that you can understand what has happened to Marni."

"What are you talking about?"

"I am talking about the Omega Protocol."

"What the hell is the Omega Protocol?"

He shook his head and sucked on the cigarette, like it might give him strength. He inhaled deep and spoke with the smoke escaping from his mouth in small clouds. "It goes back a long way, Lacklan, longer than you can imagine." He paused, shaking his head, like he couldn't believe his own thoughts. "Certain interests—let's just call them that for now—certain interests realized, a long time ago, that as a result of the Industrial Revolution, overpopulation was going to become not just a major problem, but *the* major problem on our planet."

"That's Malthus."

He nodded. "He was one of the first." He recited Malthus' proposition: "Population grows exponentially, resources grow arithmetically. Basically, population grows more and faster than food production. Of course, the Industrial Revolution meant that we were able to produce food on a scale that Malthus never dreamed possible, and capitalists crowed that Malthus had been proven wrong, that production could keep pace with population. But at the same time, the very scientific revolution that was generating food on such a vast scale was providing medical advances that were wiping out disease and increasing longevity by almost fifty percent. So as food production boomed, so also did population boom." He snorted. "Of course, back in *his* day the population of the Earth was less than one and a half billion. Today we stand at over seven and a half billion, and as Malthus predicted, it is growing almost exponentially. It seems our *obsession* as a species is to eliminate death, and extend everybody's lifespan to infinity."

I smoked and sipped my whiskey and watched him, and wondered if he had lost his mind. As though he had read mine, he glanced at me and smiled. "Don't worry, I have not gone mad. There is a relevance to all this preamble. Malthus was not the only one to harbor these concerns. There were others, among them a number of powerful industrialists and political philosophers here in the States." He paused again, staring at the fire, then said, surprisingly, "So there was that."

He heaved a big sigh and went on: "Then there was Tyndal, in the 1850s, who realized that certain gases, namely those emitted by the burning of fossil fuels, would tend to heat up the atmosphere. Unfortunately, by the time he was able to prove it, there were too many interests at stake—too many people making vast fortunes out of mining and burning those very fuels for anybody to give a damn about what Tyndall had to say."

He gave a harsh laugh and convulsed into a fit of coughing, waving his hand as though he could dismiss the hacking noise as inopportune and irrelevant.

"But by the end of the Second World War, about a hundred years later, a club had formed..."

"A club? What kind of club?"

He looked at the tip of his cigarette, breathing noisily, like he might be able to see the club there and work out what kind it was. "A very special kind of club. You might say it was unique.

It was a group of some of the most powerful men in the world, who decided, after the chaos of the three world wars, that the destiny of the world could not be left to random fate." He gave a sardonic, twisted laugh. "Democratically elected leaders, *puppets!*, pray to powerful and greedy industrialists rich enough to buy senators and even presidents. No, it had to be guided, and guided where *we* wanted it to go."

I felt a flash of irritation. "Is this some kind of conspiracy theory shit? What the fuck has this got to do with Marni?"

He looked at me under his eyebrows, as he had done many times when I was a kid, when he was about to beat me with his belt. "It is not a theory and it is not shit. These men formed what came to be known as the Government with the Government. And they, their associates and allies, controlled everything from the Federal Reserve and the media to the military industrial complex. This is *fact,* Lacklan. But from the 1950s they knew they had one major problem."

I raised an eyebrow at him. "Just one?"

He shook his head. "No, you're right. It was two, but in time they would become one." The fire spat like a firecracker and shot a shower of sparks onto the hearth. He sighed through his nose and pulled the blanket up around his waist. "They realized that sometime early in the new millennium, those two problems would come together. They had people researching it, great minds looking into it, and they realized that the Earth, our planet, could not sustain more than eight and a half or nine billion people; and, with Nature's exquisite sense of timing, just about the time we hit that number, the heating of the planet, what we are calling now climate change, would start to impact food. We would start getting widespread droughts and crop failures across vast stretches of the belly of the globe..."

"The prairie farms, the areas where all the wheat is cultivated."

"And the rice and the vegetables and the fruit and the meat—everything, Lacklan. All the world's food. We had postponed the Malthus problem, but in doing so we had turned it into a nightmare, into a holocaust in the making. Eight or nine billion starving people, with all the implications that carried with it."

I took a pull of my whiskey and shook my head while I sucked my teeth.

"It sounds like science fiction. How do you know any of this is true?"

He tossed his cigarette butt into the fire and sat staring at where the flames flared up and died away, leaving only a snake of smoke.

"Because I am a member of that club."

"*You?*"

He nodded, then looked at me. "You have no idea how powerful I am, Lacklan, the things I can do, or have done."

"How fucking rich are you? I knew you were rich, but..."

"More than you could possibly imagine. And what I have access to goes beyond even that."

"This is crazy. I don't even believe you. Why are you telling me this, Robert? What has this to do with Marni? This is bullshit!"

He scowled. "Must you call me Robert? I am your father! Whether you like it or not! If you want to rebel don't call me anything, but have some respect and don't call me Robert!"

I stared at my whiskey and repeated the question. "What has this to do with Marni?"

"Marni's father was my closest friend. Do you remember him?"

"Of course I do. Frank. We were always either at his house or they were here."

He smiled, not at me but at the memory. "You and Marni were like brother and sister. Closer than that. As you got older, we always believed you and she would get married. Maybe that would have been the best thing."

"You're rambling. What's the point of all this?"

"Do you remember Frank's job? You remember what he did?"

I frowned and thought about it. "He was a professor at Harvard."

"Do you recall his specialization?"

I sighed and cast my mind back. I had been very young, six or seven. The fire crackled again and the warmth made me sleepy. It had been a long drive.

"Yeah, it was something to do with Earth Sciences, the environment. He was a devotee of Lovelock's..."

He was watching me, nodding. "Exactly. His research had proved conclusively that by the middle of the next decade drought and famine were going to sweep across the globe. Hundreds of millions, possibly billions of people, were going to die of starvation and disease. He was predicting that this would lead to a refugee crisis on an unprecedented scale that would make the Syrian crisis look like a picnic. He predicted war, the unbridled rise of tyrannical regimes and Islam, and a humanitarian cataclysm of unimaginable proportions." He paused. "He was preparing to present his findings to the United Nations and the international press."

I pulled another cigarette from the pack and lit up. I inhaled deeply and squinted at him through the smoke. "So what happened?"

"I was instructed to kill him."

I sat forward, "*What?*"

"He was aware of us, of our existence. He had to be, in his position, doing the work he was doing. I advised him several times that what he was proposing to reveal was contrary to our plans. That we had it covered. That he should desist. But he refused. He insisted on going ahead with his plan. In the end he left us no choice."

"You killed your closest friend?"

"That is what I am telling you."

I stared at him, shaking my head, "What... What *are* you? What kind of sick monster...?"

He spoke quietly, to the fire. "That is not the issue now. The priority now is Marni."

I shook my head again. "No. I should leave."

"If you do, Marni will die as surely as the sun will rise tomorrow. As surely as her father died twenty-three years ago."

"You sick fuck."

"Get it out of your system, I have a lot more to tell you."

"You sick *fuck!*"

"You done?" He waited. I didn't say anything, so he went on. "He knew it was coming. He accepted it. He was not resentful. I did it myself and I made sure it was painless. Before he died he asked me a favor, and I have honored that request.

He asked me to take care of his daughter as though she were my own, and to make sure no harm came to her."

I struggled to understand what he was telling me. "Are you trying to justify what you did?"

"No. I don't expect you to understand, and I don't need or want your forgiveness. But what I do need is for you to understand that not a day has gone by since Frank's death that I have not regretted his killing. I loved Frank more than a brother. And he knew that. But now Marni is threatening to do the same as her father."

"How?"

"You lost touch with her. That was stupid, Lacklan. You let your screwed-up relationship with me ruin your relationship with her. That was stupid."

"Mind your own fucking business."

He gave me a sour look but went on. "The point is, you wouldn't know because you turned your back on her. Just as I killed my best friend, you turned your back on yours. She went into the same field as Frank, and proved to be just as brilliant as he was."

"What happened to his research?"

"It was never found. We searched the whole house, his office... We looked everywhere. It was never found. But it seems possible that Marni may have found it. Whatever the case may be, I know Omega went after her. They didn't tell me, they knew I would have opposed them. But either she has been abducted, or she got wind of the threat somehow, because she has vanished without a trace."

I was silent for a long while, listening to the bizarrely comfortable crackle of the fire, and the long, complicated song of the blackbird outside the French windows. My heart was thumping hard, and I could feel my hand shaking on the arm of the chair.

"Have they killed her?"

"No."

"How do you know?"

"They would inform me." He said it to the hot embers of the fire. "It's protocol, and they are great believers in protocol. They either have her, alive, or they are looking for her."

"What do you want from me?"

He turned his old head to face me. It was bathed in firelight and I could see small flames dancing in his eyes. It made him look diabolical.

"I want you to do for her what I should have done twenty-three years ago for Frank. I want you to make her safe. Find her, and protect her."

There was a tap on the door. Kenny stepped in. "Dinner is served, sir."

My father studied me a moment and said, "Stay. We've still got a lot to talk about."

Three

THE DINING ROOM WAS large, with a high ceiling in the Georgian style. With my father sitting hunched at the end of the long, Queen Anne dining table, it looked cheerless and very cavernous. He had always been a man who filled a room just by being in it, with his massive presence and huge personality. Now the room seemed to crush him with its emptiness. There was a place set on his right. He gestured to it and after a moment I sat.

"I'm the guest of honor when there's nobody else, huh?"

He ignored me and shook out his napkin with his left hand. That's what you're taught to do when you're a Boston Brahmin. "There was a time we used to dress for dinner," he said. "Those things are not considered important anymore."

"Was that before or after you murdered your best friend?"

He stared bitterly at some vague point on the tabletop. "At the same time," he said. "That was all at the same time."

The door opened and Kenny came in with a pretty young maid in a blue and white uniform. She had a tray with a meat pie on it, and a couple of dishes with potatoes, Brussels sprouts and carrots. She set it on the sideboard and began to serve us, while Kenny poured the wine.

When they had gone, he started eating. He ate greedily and with concentrated focus, shoveling forkfuls of food into his mouth. I sipped my wine and watched him.

"What happened?"

"Her mother died when she had just turned twenty."

"Was that anything to do with you?"

"Of course not." He dabbed his mouth and drained his glass. As he refilled it he said, "We were close. She—Marni—used to come over two or three times a week. We'd dine. She'd tell me about her work. She always talked about you. Unlike me, she was never bitter or resentful about the fact that you dumped her."

"Why would *you* be resentful? And anyway, I didn't *dump* her."

He waved a hand at me, as though my words were flies that were annoying him. "She was not like family, she *is* family. Like my own daughter. Last week I didn't hear from her. So I took a walk over there."

"She kept on her mother's house?"

He shrugged. "She could afford it. And I guess she wanted to stay close. You and Bob were like brothers... *are* like brothers to her. I guess she saw me as a kind of surrogate father."

"She was lucky to have you..." I couldn't keep the bitterness from my voice. I didn't even try. He sighed, stuffed some more food in his maw and carried on, talking with his mouth full, illustrating each point with a wave of his knife.

"So... when I didn't hear from her I walked over to her house. There was post in her mailbox. Her car was not in the driveway. The drapes were drawn in the drawing room, but I walked 'round and looked in at the library and the kitchen windows. I don't know how to explain it, but it didn't look as though she had gone away." He narrowed his eyes, gazing at the tabletop. "There were dirty plates by the sink, a newspaper open on her favorite chair..."

I nodded.

He shrugged. "Yet she hadn't been in touch for almost a week."

"What did you do?"

"I called the police. I had to pull some strings, but they asked the Sheriff's Department to send over a deputy. I have a key, so we went in and had a look around. Her toothbrush was gone, and so was her toothpaste, but everything else was as though she were still there. I found Anita's number..."

"Anita?"

"The girl who cleans for her. I called her and she said Marni had paid her the month in advance and told her she was going to be away for a few days. She'd contact her when she got back."

"You tried her cell?"

"Of course. Switched off."

"Would she have told you if..."

"She told me everything, Lacklan." He gave me a sour look. "I was a better friend to her than you were. If she was going away for a few days, for work or on a break—*whatever*—she would have told me."

The barb stung, but I ignored it. "So what are you thinking?"

He puffed out his cheeks and blew loudly, then glanced at my food. "You're not eating."

"I'm not hungry."

He pulled over my plate and started eating my meal. "She's either on the run or she's been abducted."

"That's a pretty big jump."

He shook his head, chewed and swallowed while loading up his fork. "No, it's not. Not if you have listened to a damn word I have said. For the last couple of years she had been following up her father's research, working in the same areas and on the same theses."

I suddenly went cold. Spiders' legs seemed to crawl across my scalp. I narrowed my eyes at him. "Jesus! Did *you*...?"

He scowled at me. "No! Of course not!" He turned back to his plate, shoveling food into his mouth. "I kept warning her of the dangers, as much as I could, but she has the same kind of idealistic pig-headedness as her father... and as you."

"Don't kid yourself."

"Omega warned me to stop her, and I tried, hinted heavily. But she wouldn't listen, and..." He wiped his mouth with his napkin, picked up his glass and drained it. "I think maybe she found her father's notes. I think maybe he left her some kind of message, somehow, some clue, telling her where to look."

I curled my lip. "And you want me to find her for you, so you can kill her."

He pounded the table with his fist, making the knives and forks jump. His face flushed red and tears stood out in his eyes.

"*Enough!*" He stared at me and his hands were shaking on the table. "You are not *helping* her with this attitude! Try to get past your personal prejudice and your hatred! *She needs you!* And the only way you can help her is through *me!*"

"Give me one reason—*just one!*—why I should believe *anything* that you say!"

"I can't. I haven't got one. All I can tell you is that I regret the things I have had to do in my life. I wish it hadn't fallen to me to do them. But it did. When you are in an overcrowded lifeboat, *somebody* has to decide who lives and who gets thrown overboard, otherwise everybody dies. And somebody has to do the throwing." He stared at his glass, breathing heavily. "People like me make the decisions. And people like you do the throwing." He slumped back in his chair and looked at me with something close to contempt. "Besides, when you are done passing judgment, ask yourself, what fucking choice have you got?"

He was right, on both counts, and I knew it. I, who killed people for a living, had no place passing judgment on him. And further more, I had no choice but to accept what he told me. I could not walk away from Marni. If she was in trouble, I had to help her. Walking away was not an option.

"So what did the deputy make of it?"

"Nothing. I pulled strings and had a detective and a crime scene team go over the house. But forty-eight hours into the investigation, it was stopped and Omega told me to butt out or face the consequences. Either they have her, or they are searching for her."

"So you sent for me."

He searched my face. "Did I do the right thing?"

I nodded. "Yeah. You did the right thing."

He refilled his glass and pushed over the decanter. "I want you to go and have a look at the house, and I want you to talk to Detective Mendelson. He conducted what investigation there was."

"What about Omega? Won't that get back to them?"

He shrugged. "Maybe. I can tell them it's something you are doing on your own account. First they'll try to stonewall you. If you keep pushing they will come after you. It is high risk, you understand that."

"Yes."

"They will try to kill you."

"I get it."

For a moment he looked embarrassed. "I... There isn't a lot more I can do to help. But..." He reached into the inside pocket of his smoking jacket and pulled out an envelope. He opened it and extracted a black AMEX card and a slip of paper. He handed me that first. There were two names and two phone numbers. One, Philip Gantrie, was in Arizona, the other, Borg Olafsen, was in New York.

"These two men will help you if you need them. They are good people and they owe me. I have told them that at some point you may contact them..."

"I don't need them."

"Don't let your stupidity and your arrogance get in the way of helping Marni, Lacklan. Don't be an asshole all your fucking life. Phil is a nerd. He is a genius and he can help you with anything that is technical: IT, electronics... You may need him. And Olafsen is the most dangerous man I have ever met. He went from the Seals to the CIA and is now a private contractor. He is one of the five best assassins in the business. If you don't need them, fine. But if you do, they are there. They will help you."

He waited. I didn't say anything so he dropped the AMEX on the table in front of me. "This draws on a black account. It is not American Express. It's untraceable, even to Omega. It leaves no footprint. The account, to all intents and purposes, does not exist."

"I don't need your money."

"I won't tell you again, Lacklan. You need all the resources you can get if you are going to help her. Now take it."

I put the card in my wallet and memorized the names and the numbers, then burnt them.

"I'll take a walk down to the house tomorrow morning. Then I'll go and see Mendelson."

"He's a good man. He'll want to help."

I went to stand.

"Lacklan..."

"What?"

He looked away from me. His face was contorted for a moment. He was frowning, like he was trying to understand something.

"I haven't been a good father."

"That's not true." He looked at me in surprise. "You were a great father, for Bob and for Marni. You were just a shit father for me, and a shit husband for Mom."

He looked away again. "You are determined to punish me."

"You remember what you always used to say to me when I was a kid? To Bob you always used to say, 'You can do it, Bob! You can do anything you put your mind to!' To me you used to say, 'You made your bed, Lacklan, now you have to lie in it.' Well, *Dad*, you made your fucking bed, now you can lie in it."

I left him there, sitting, hunched and small at that ancient table, and made my way upstairs to my room. I found it exactly as I had last left it, over thirteen years earlier.

Four

I WAS UP AT FIVE AND went for a long run in the woods and to spar with some trees. They make great opponents: however hard you hit them, they never go down. At six, I went to see Rosalia in the kitchen. She'd been my father's cook for thirty years and had seen me grow up from a skinny, disobedient kid into—into whatever it was I had become.

After she'd squealed, pinched my cheeks and smothered me in kisses, she sat me down at the table and made me the best bacon and fried bananas in the world, and the best Colombian coffee. While I was eating, she sat with me and kept grabbing my hand and pinching my face, which made it hard to get on with the task in hand. But it was nice. It almost felt like being home.

After a bit she looked said and asked me, "You gonna find Marni?"

I nodded. "Yeah."

"*Tu papaíto*, he really miss her, you know?" I drank my coffee and didn't answer. She gave a smile that was eloquent of sadness and gripped my hand. "He really miss you too. I know you don' belief it. But is true."

I shrugged. "*Mucha historia, Rosalía.*"

She threw her hands in the air. "Sure! Lots of history in every family! But what you gonna do in life, more important than make peace with your family?"

I gave her a kiss and stood. "Right now, find Marni."

She gripped me in a tight hug. "*Ay!* Do that, and you make your daddy very happy, and me."

I gave her another kiss, on the top of her head. "And me."

I took the back route through the woods. It was the way we used to go when we were kids. Where our land joined with theirs, there was a dry stone wall—or rather, there had been one once—but it had decayed and crumbled with the years. And quietly, unobtrusively, Frank and Silvia's land had melded with ours. That meld had been a simple expression of the fusion between our two families, especially after Frank died and my parents divorced.

I had wondered in later years if there had ever been anything between Silvia and my father. If there had been, they had kept it quiet. But I was never quite sure.

I clambered over the crumbling, mossy wall and continued under the beech and chestnut trees until. Here and there a twig cracked, wings flapped in the canopy above, a crow cawed in the early mist.

Eventually I came to the fringe of the woods, fifteen or twenty yards from the back of the house. There I lay on my belly and stayed motionless for twenty minutes, watching and listening. Apart from the birds and the squirrels, there was nothing.

When I was satisfied I was alone, I rose and walked to the back door that opened into the kitchen and peered through the windows. As my father had said, there was a dirty plate and a cup by the sink. There was also a book, a mug and some mail on the large pine table that stood at the centre of the room. I spent the next hour wandering around the surrounding woodlands, examining the undergrowth and the turf. Then I walked up and down the driveway.

I didn't find anything in the woods. But I found something on the driveway. It was mostly gravel, though there was one patch on the bend where the gravel had been worn away by the recurrent passage of vehicles, and the dirt had been revealed beneath. There I saw two tire marks, one overlaid on the other, each with a different print. The first was hard to make out, but it looked like a small car. The one that had gone over it was a big SUV. I thought I recognized it as a Q7. I pulled out my cell and took a photograph.

Then I made my way down to the house and let myself in with my father's key. The house wasn't as grand as ours. Frank had been a very successful Harvard professor, so he had made a lot of money lecturing and writing books. He also came from old money; but my father was a very successful son of a bitch who made his money by legal extortion, political manipulation, and exploiting people in weaker positions than himself. And he was extremely good at all that. He came from a long line of Boston Brahmins, and he had married an English aristocrat. All of these things gave him an edge in life.

In a universe where we have to eat each other in order to survive, it pays to have no soul, and the instincts of a cannibal.

I stood in a large, silent hallway. Silvia's study—or what I had grown up thinking of as Silvia's study, but was now Marni's—was on the right. The drawing room was on the left. Behind it, separated by louvered doors, was the dining room, with tall French windows out onto the formal garden and the dark woods. Beyond the study were the games room, the breakfast room, and the kitchen. In the centre of the hall stood the broad staircase, rising like a pair of ram's horns to the galleried landing and the bedrooms.

It was all quite formal and understated. My mother used to say it was painfully upper-middle class. Her English friends used to laugh when she said things like that. Her American ones didn't know what she was talking about but pretended to be amused. One always had to be amused.

I realized I had been standing there for several minutes, not so much lost in memories as living them. I'd been nineteen the last time I had walked through that door. I had come to say goodbye to Silvia, and to Marni. They had no butler, so Silvia had opened the door to me herself, and led me through to the drawing room. They had both listened to me, serious and quiet, until I'd finished explaining. Then Marni had run from the room, stomping up the stairs, and Silvia had asked me to think very carefully about what I was doing, and what I was throwing away.

I crossed the hall. Ours was tiled, theirs was old, stained wood. It creaked slightly under my feet and echoed in the vast silence of the house. The drawing room was sunlit, bright compared to the gloom of the hall. It hadn't changed much. Most of the furniture was the same. My mother had said it was eclectic. Antiques mixed in with expensive modern stuff. Large slabs of sunlight lay across the Persian rug. Marni's chair, the one that had been her mother's favorite, had a *New York Times* open on it, crumpled as though thrown down suddenly while going to do something else. I picked it up and looked at the page she had been reading. It was the science page. The rate of Greenland's melt had been underestimated—again. There were fears of drought in the Ukraine.

I threw it back down on the chair and looked around. The room didn't tell me anything, except that it wasn't the room of a person who has decided to go away for an extended period.

I climbed the stairs to the upper floor. There were five bedrooms, and all but one of them were obviously unoccupied. They had bare mattresses on the beds, covered in dust sheets. In her room the bed had been slept in and left unmade. The duvet was thrown back and the sheet was rumpled. In the bathroom, as my father had said, her toothbrush was missing, as was the toothpaste. Her hairbrush was also gone. I looked around for her tampons. I found the cupboard where she would have kept them, but there weren't any there.

So, there had been a last minute decision to go away for a prolonged period. I checked through her drawers and her wardrobe. There were no pants, no bras, and no socks. But there were other clothes.

I sat on the bed and wondered where she had decided to go. And, perhaps more to the point, what had made her decide. I allowed the images to arise in my imagination. She was sitting in her chair, reading the *Times*. Something happened. Something made her get up and dump the paper.

I thought of the kitchen, of the letter on the table. The postman? Or had that been before she went to read the paper? I frowned. The sequence of events was wrong. Wouldn't you read the paper over breakfast?

I went down to the kitchen.

It was a broad, ample space with windows above the sink that gave views of an herb garden and the woods about twenty or thirty yards away. There was a deep blue Rayburn cooker on the left, and a long, heavy pine table in the middle of the stone-flagged floor. A half-empty bottle of washing up liquid glowed green on the windowsill. For the moment, I ignored the table and went to the sink.

There was a plate and a knife. They both had traces of butter and maple syrup on them, and crumbs, probably from pancakes. Next to the plate there was a small espresso cup on a saucer, with dried coffee stains on it.

That was breakfast, probably taken at six or seven A.M., *before* the paper arrived.

Now I turned and looked at the table. At the head there was a placemat. The chair had been pulled out and angled slightly and by the mat there was a pen and a book of *New York Times* cryptic crosswords. I felt a warm pellet of adrenaline as I remembered the way she used to sit at breakfast, doing the crossword, with her right leg slung over her left, biting her pen. I was willing to bet that was where she sat every morning for breakfast.

But two places down, on the near side, that chair had also been pulled out, and there was a mug there that still had coffee in it. Beside the mug there was an envelope, the one I had seen from the window. I stepped over and picked it up.

It was printed and addressed to her by name: Ms Marni Gilbert. The postmark was downtown Boston. There was no letter inside it. I did a tour of the kitchen, pulled out the trash and went through it item by item. It hadn't been thrown away, at least not here. Then I went over the whole house, searching for the letter in every conceivable place. I even checked the fireplace for ash. Neither the letter nor its remains were in the house. Eventually I went back to the kitchen, made myself some coffee and sat opposite where she had sat to read it. I allowed my imagination to recreate the events.

She'd been having a lazy morning. She'd had an early breakfast in the kitchen—she was always an early riser—pancakes and maple syrup while doing a crossword. When the paper had arrived she'd risen, collected it and gone to the drawing room, where she had sat in her favorite chair reading the article about the melting of Greenland.

Then the postman had arrived. She'd heard him and got up from her chair, dumped the paper and gone down the path to get the letters from the mail box. Among them she had found a letter—not just a bill or an official notification, but an actual letter. A rare occurrence in these days of e-mails. So she'd taken it to the kitchen, to make a second cup of coffee, and sat down to read it.

And whatever she had read had made her decide her to leave, immediately, without letting anyone know except Anita, her cleaner. That made sense, even if she had wanted to disappear. If she hadn't given her some kind of explanation, Anita would have alerted the cops and started a search in earnest. This way there was no official cause to go looking for her.

But that raised the question, what stopped her from phoning my father and telling *him* she was going away? I could only think of two reasons. A: she was trying to protect him somehow; B: she was running from him.

I found a plastic sandwich bag, slipped the envelope into it and put it in my pocket. Then I went out and opened the garage. My father had told me that she had a blue Honda Civic, but there had been no car keys in the house, and there was no car in the garage. So she'd left in her vehicle. And *after* that a large SUV had arrived. Maybe the cops.

Maybe.

Four

I CALLED DETECTIVE Mendelson and he agreed to see me if I could make it within the hour. I told him I could make it in half an hour. I walked back through the woods, climbed in my car and headed down to Weston, through the early autumn woodlands, in absolute silence. Fifteen minutes later I pulled up in the parking lot outside the big, friendly, blue and white cop shop and stepped inside to tell the desk sergeant I wanted to see Mendelson. She gave me a friendly smile and asked me to take a seat while she called him. Then she offered me coffee. Cops in Weston are not like cops anywhere else.

Mendelson arrived two minutes later and shook my hand.

"Walk and talk," he said, as he held the door open for me.

I followed him across the parking lot to the State Bypass and we started strolling east into town.

"You said your name was Lacklan Walker?" I nodded. "It's an unusual name. You must be Robert Walker's son."

"Yeah."

"I can understand why you're concerned about Ms Gilbert. It's certainly out of character for her to take off like that. But, like I told your father, there is no indication of a crime having been committed, and the fact that she gave her cleaner time off, kind of suggests it was voluntary, and she knew what she was doing. So really there are no grounds for the police to get involved." He looked at me curiously as we crossed onto Colpitts

Road. "What is your interest in this, Mr. Walker? I understand you've been out of the country for about ten years."

"Yeah. I was in England." I shrugged. "My interest? Marni and I grew up together. She was like a sister. We'd lost touch, but when my father told me she'd disappeared without telling him... It felt wrong."

He nodded once. "She's a lecturer at Harvard, right?"

"Yeah. Did you contact the university?"

He took a deep breath and let it out slowly through his nose. "Did you?"

I was a bit surprised by his answer. "Not yet. I only arrived last night."

He didn't say anything for a bit until we turned onto the Boston Post Road, which in Weston is like the High Street.

"I did contact them," he said, "and her department head said he was aware that she had taken some time off, and they had no reason to think there was anything amiss. So, I'm kind of curious as to why you and your father are so sure something is wrong."

"Like you said, it's out of character. Also," I shook my head, "It doesn't quite jive. She'd had her breakfast and was reading the paper in the drawing room..." I watched his face as I spoke. "She received a letter, took it to the kitchen to read it over coffee, and then immediately packed up, called her cleaner—but not my father—and left. Apparently she called the university too. So..." I shrugged again. "Why *not* my father, who was like a second father to her?"

He shrugged. "Any number of reasons—a lover, a boyfriend, somebody she didn't want your father to know about. It's like that sometimes, especially in a father-daughter relationship." He grinned. "I should know. I have three daughters."

We'd come to a café-cum-pizza restaurant. He stopped and pushed open the door for me. We went in and he ordered coffee and blueberry pie. I ordered coffee and we sat at a blue Formica table by the window. I sipped as he wolfed his pie.

"I haven't got any kids, Detective, but I know Marni. She is not impulsive or rash. She is grounded and very smart. She would only behave like this if something was wrong. The letter she received is nowhere in the house. Her pants are gone, her bras are gone. So are her socks and her tampons. The bed is unmade and the washing up was not done. She didn't arrange for Anita to come in, clean up and then not come back for a week or two. She paid her to the end of the month, and put her off for an indefinite time. You and I both know it's because of what was in that letter." He watched me with interest and chewed. I watched him back and asked, "What vehicle did you use when you went to the house?"

"Ford Focus, why?"

"Anybody go there with a big SUV?"

He shook his head. "Not that I know of. Why?"

I showed him the photograph of the tire marks. "After she left in her Honda Civic, somebody went down there in a big SUV."

He looked at the photograph and handed it back. "Strange behavior does not constitute grounds for a police investigation, Mr. Walker. If it did, New England police would be swamped. Academics are notoriously eccentric."

I sighed. "I understand that, Detective, but maybe you can help me anyway."

He looked up from his pie with eyes like scalpels. "How?"

I sat back and watched him a moment. "How long have you been on the force, Detective Mendelson, twenty years?"

"There abouts."

"So I'm wondering, why does a cop with your experience waste time on a guy like me who is chasing shadows looking for a girl who just went away for a week of debauchery in Hawaii? Why the walk and talk? You could have told me what you've told me in two minutes on the phone and had lunch with your wife, or one of your three daughters."

He smiled, finished his pie and sat back, holding his coffee cup like a glass of beer. "What's your point?"

"You're as curious about this case as I am. But I am curious because I knew Marni like I know myself. What's your reason? What has made you curious?"

He nodded several times, then sat forward and put down his cup without drinking from it. "OK, I'll tell you. I've been expecting you to turn up." I raised an eyebrow at him. "I know who you are. Everybody in Weston knows who you are. Your dad is the big shot and we all know how he stepped in and helped the Gilberts after Frank died. And we all thought you and Marni would get married. It's a small town. You guys are our celebrities, our own, living soap opera. But then you went off to England, and we thought we'd seen the last of you. You passed out of village gossip."

"You're losing me."

He reached in his pocket and pulled out his wallet. From among his cards, he extracted a photograph and dropped it on the table in front of me. It was a picture of Marni. She was smiling into the camera, squinting slightly because of the sun. All you could see behind her was pine forest. It had been printed out on a computer, and there was a broad white border under the picture, where she had written 'Lack.'

"It was pinned to her cork notice board in the kitchen." He gave a small shrug. "Call it a hunch, like in the movies, but my gut told me there was probably only one person in the whole world, besides her, who knew where that picture had been taken. That's your name written at the bottom, right? She figured you'd turn up before long, asking questions. Maybe she didn't tell your dad, because she wanted him to worry. Maybe she figured if he worried, he'd call on you. Keep it. I didn't see it, I didn't find it and I didn't give it to you."

I slipped it into my own wallet. "Thanks, but that still doesn't explain..."

He was shaking his head. "There is something else. Within an hour of phoning the university, I got a call from the colonel's office..."

"The colonel?"

"The supreme commander of the Massachusetts State Police. His office called and instructed me to drop any investigation, and not to discuss her disappearance with anybody, under any circumstances. So that made me curious."

"What reason did they give?"

"The reasons I have given you. Her job was notoriously stressful. She was a young woman. She probably needed to get away. A scandal in the papers could damage her career." He sat back and spread his hands. "All valid points, but as far as I am aware the colonel's office does not intervene in that kind of thing. The only way that could have happened was if your father had pulled strings. But I knew he hadn't, because he was the one asking me to investigate."

I nodded. "Two gets you twenty, whoever pulled strings at the colonel's office, drives a large SUV."

He shrugged. "All I can tell you, Mr. Walker, is that the police cannot investigate unless there is actual evidence of a crime. And at the moment there is none." He studied my face. "Do you know where it is? Where the photograph was taken?"

I shook my head. "No."

But he knew I was lying and smiled. "Good."

I stood. "Thank you, Detective. I guess the best thing I can do now is go back to Wyoming."

"I guess you're right."

We shook hands and I left.

I found my father seated in front of the fire in the drawing room, with his red tartan blanket over his knees. He watched me come in and sit in the burgundy chesterfield armchair opposite him.

"Did you find anything?"

I shook my head. "No."

Like Mendelson, he knew I was lying. "What are you going to do?"

"Go back to Wyoming."

He looked troubled. I told myself I didn't care. "What about Marni?"

I shrugged. "I guess she'll turn up when you least expect her."

A spasm of pain flashed across his face. "Lacklan, son..."

I shook my head. "Don't. It's too late for that." I stood. "You made your bed, now you have to lie in it. Remembr?"

In the hall I found Ben coming down the stairs. He smiled without feeling in his pale blue eyes. "Glad you could make it. Will you be staying long?"

I shook my head. "I'm leaving now."

I went down to the kitchen and said goodbye to Kenny and Rosalia. Rosalia wanted to know when I would come back. I told her soon, but we all three knew that next time I came to that house, it would be for my father's funeral.

Five

IT WAS A THIRTY HOUR drive, back along the I-90 and the I-80; and then the I-76 from Big Springs to Denver. After Denver it was a three-hour, winding climb on Highway 285, up into the remotest part of the Rockies, where there is no black-top on the roads, and no street view on Google Earth, to a town called Turret.

When we were kids, Turret was a ghost town: a handful of semi-derelict shacks that had once been people's homes, back in the days when men were men and so were women. Silvia, Marni's mother, had bought and partly restored a cabin out in the foothills of Green Mountain, a mile or so from the town. She was a sensitive, artistic woman, and liked to go there and paint. For a few years, till we were eleven or twelve, each August during the holidays we would spend a couple of weeks or three playing at Daniel Boone and Davy Crockett among the mountains and forests. Then we stopped going, until the summer before I went to England. Then, aged eighteen, Marni and I had come out here alone. That was when I took the picture.

Now Turret was not a ghost town anymore. It was coming back to life. There was a bar that looked like an old time saloon. Now it was closed because it only opened in the summer months, but there was a diner, a post office, a general store and a whole cluster of new houses. I figured maybe there were a dozen new homes.

It was midday when I parked in front of the diner and stepped inside. It was empty, but there was a pretty girl behind the counter washing glasses. She smiled as I came in.

"Oh, boy!" She said it like I should know what she was talking about. "A new face!"

I smiled. "Your face is new to me, too." I sat on a stool at the bar. "Can I get a beer and a burger?"

"Fries?"

I nodded. "Are you going to let me smoke?"

"For all I care, you can burst into flames, pal. Last time I seen the sheriff 'round here, I wasn't even born!"

She cracked me a beer and went into the kitchen. I peeled a pack of Camel, extracted a butt and poked it in my mouth, speaking around the cigarette as I leaned into the flame of my Zippo.

"I guess you don't get many strangers 'round here."

"Only people who come here, Mister," she called over the hiss of the griddle, "are either working on the farm, lost, or they're crazy."

I smiled. "Which one are you?"

She peered out and grinned. "I am both lost *and* crazy. And I was going to ask you the same question."

"Well, I guess I'm crazy. Used to come out here when I was a kid. We had a cabin out on North Spring Road. Haven't been there for over ten years. Just had a sudden hankering to see it again."

She came out and leaned on the bar. "You from New York?" I shook my head. She had an infectious smile. "You talk funny."

I smiled back. "Y'all do too."

She winked. "That's two things we got in common."

"I'm sure if we looked we could find more."

She giggled and disappeared back into the kitchen. Five minutes later she returned with a man-sized burger in a bun and enough fries to feed a retreating French army.

"I guess I looked hungry."

She leaned her ass against the cash register and folded a piece of gum into her mouth. "You look like a man who'd have an appetite."

"I might be. Speaking of which, where can I get a bed around here?"

"You ain't shy, I'll say that."

I bit into the burger and chewed, watching her. She watched me back with amused insolence in her eyes. I said, "So?"

"We got a couple of rooms upstairs."

"I'll take one."

"Ten bucks a night. Food's extra."

I finished my burger, paid her five nights in advance and took the Zombie up North Spring Road.

Like I said, there was no blacktop up here, and as I wound my way deeper into the mountains I was pursued by a vast cloud of billowing dust that never quite seemed to catch me. After about a mile, I came to a rough, dirt track on the right and followed it for half a mile, climbing through dense pine woods. Three or four hundred yards up, a second track branched off through the forest onto a flat glade. That was where the cabin stood. Just beyond it the woods swept down into a deep, dense gorge. Behind it, they climbed toward the peak.

There was no car there, but I didn't expect there to be. She would have concealed it somewhere and come up by foot, staying among the trees, among the shadows. I mounted the steps to the porch and peered through the window. It was dark inside and I couldn't see much. I tried the door. It was open.

It was one room, neat and clean, with an open fire, an iron range and a sink. A dining table stood in the middle of the floor, and against the far wall there was a sofa, a chair and a TV. In back there was a bedroom and a toilet.

I checked the toilet and found her toothbrush and her tampons. In the bedroom I found her pants and her bras, a couple of pairs of jeans, some sweatshirts and a pair of boots; but not her.

Back in the living room I picked up a notepad and a pen and sat at the table. I thought for a moment, then remembered a hideout we used to go to, near the peak at the back of the house. We'd called it the Hole in the Wall, after Billy the Kid's hide out. I made a rough sketch of it and signed it Billy. In our games, I was always Billy and she was Pat Garrett. I left it on the table and stepped outside.

I spent the next four hours exploring the woods above the cabin. I found her tracks but nobody else's, and knew that she'd probably gone to the hideout. I didn't follow her there. She would tell me when it was OK to meet. Instead, once I knew she was alive, I made my way to the car and drove back to Turret. By the time I got there, the sun was sinking behind the peaks in the west and there were a couple of trucks parked outside the diner.

I pushed in and made my way to the bar. There were maybe a dozen guys sitting at various tables drinking beer and talking about the kind of things guys talk about—things that are roughly spherical: balls, breasts and backsides. I climbed on a stool and my pretty waitress came to me.

"Find what you were looking for, Mr. Crazy?"

"Just right now."

She narrowed her eyes and pointed a finger at me like a gun. "You are a smooth talker, Mister, an' I don't trust that in a man."

"Well now that you mistrust me, why don't you tell me your name?"

"What's yours?"

"Lacklan."

"Lacklan? What kind of name is that?"

"A very ancient one. It means Viking Invader. How about you?"

There was a sparkle of humor in her eyes. "Don't you laugh, y'hear? It's Blueberry. Bluberry MacDonald."

"Well, Blueberry, I guess that makes you edible. So, to stop this Viking invader from going right ahead and eating you, why don't you give me a beer and make me a steak and fries?"

She squealed a laugh, cracked me a beer and went into the kitchen area. I sensed a hush and looked around. One of the tables had gone quiet and there was a big redneck turned around in his chair to look at me. I'm not small. I'm six-one, but this guy was six-three easy and built like two brick shithouses. I looked back at the bar and took a swig.

I heard Man Mountain McCoy get up and walk slowly to the bar where he leaned beside me.

"Hey! Blueberry! What I godda do to get a beer 'round here?"

Her voice came over the sound of frying meat. "How about wait?"

He leaned on one elbow and looked me over. "Well how come this bozo din' have to wait?"

She leaned out of the kitchen. "Shut up, Earl. Sit down an' I'll bring you your beer when I'm done."

"Well, I don't think that's very nice, Blueberry. I see you laughing with this streak a'piss, giving him most anything *he* wants, and when I talk to you, you tell me to go sit down an' wait. That ain't polite. I think you're getting a hot pussy for this guy. An' that makes me kind of jealous."

"Earl! Go and sit down before I get mad with you!"

Before he could answer I turned on my stool to face him. "Are you trying to pick a fight with me?"

"Oh now, I wouldn't go so far as to say a fight. But I can see I might have to slap you around some before the night is out."

"Just you, or are your friends going to help you?"

He grinned. "Hell no. They just gonna watch."

"That's a mistake, Earl. You're going to need help. Because first I'm going to break your right arm, then I am going to break your jaw." I got up off the stool. "Let's go outside and do it now, before my steak's done." I saw his lip curl and raised a hand. "Outside."

I stepped out onto the dark, dirt road. Earl and his three pals came out after me. They were all the size of small trucks. The drinkers from the other tables followed and stood on the porch to watch. Rednecks enjoy few things more than a good fight. I didn't plan to disappoint them. Earl and his friends surrounded me. I looked at them in turn, calibrating them.

"You reckon four of you is going to be enough?"

He snarled. "I'm gonna take you on my own, city boy." As he said it he did exactly what I knew he was going to do. He swung his huge right fist in an arc aimed roughly at my head. I leaned back as it passed, grabbed his wrist with my right hand and twisted violently forward, locking his elbow. As I did it I slammed my forearm savagely into the joint. I heard it snap and felt his shoulder pop. He screamed like a woman and staggered. I stepped around in front of him and put the fingers of my left hand on his clavicle to line him up. His arm was sticking out at a grotesque angle. His eyes were bulging at me and his mouth was open, gasping. That was what I needed. If you want to break a jaw, you need the mouth open and slack.

The right cross smashed into the left side of his mandible and broke the joint on both sides. His eyes rolled up and his legs folded under him. It took his mates two whole seconds to react. Then it was a disorganized charge. The biggest one was on my left. He was a huge mule of a guy with massive shoulders and a head like a cinderblock. He was the most aggressive too—he was the first to move, roaring that I was a dead motherfucker.

I sidestepped to my left, so he stood between me and the other two. He faltered in his charge and turned to reach for me, which left his legs bent and vulnerable. I palmed his forearm and kicked him hard in the side of the knee. I felt it crunch and snap. His face contracted with pain and he leaned forward instinctively, reaching for the shattered joint with his hands. As he did that I smashed my right elbow into the top of his skull. Maybe I'd killed him. I didn't know and I didn't care.

Now his pals had to step over him to reach me. The first was a tall, rangy guy who was fast on his feet. He was the most dangerous. So as he jumped over his fallen friend I snap-kicked him in the balls with my instep. He went down on his knees and I was happy to leave him there for now. The last of the four suddenly realized he was on his own. It was just him and me. He didn't like the odds and pulled a knife from his pocket.

I shook my head. "You shouldn't have done that. Now I'm going to kill you."

I could see in his eyes that he knew it. But he could not back down now. I reached down to my boot for my fighting knife, knowing he would lunge. He did. It was a clumsy rush and he didn't even see my blade. The first thing he was aware of was that he couldn't move his hand because the tendons in his wrist had been severed. Then the blood started spraying from the gashed veins. And that was the last thing he was ever aware of, because I had stepped behind him, grabbed his forehead and slipped the blade between the first and second vertebrae in his neck.

The guy with the busted nuts was still kneeling. So I kicked him in the back of the head.

The men on the porch watched in silence as I climbed the steps and went inside. Blueberry was waiting behind the bar. She looked surprised to see me, maybe pleased too. "What the hell did you do?"

My steak was on the bar, next to my beer. I climbed back on my stool.

"Best you don't know." I picked up the knife and fork and cut into the meat. It was perfect. "These guys work on the farm?" I asked. She nodded. "Tell me about the farm."

Six

THE DINER WAS EMPTY, so I took my plate to a table and told Blueberry to get a beer for herself and join me. She sat opposite while I ate and said, "What's to tell? The farm is the only reason this town ain't a ghost town anymore. It's the only employer there is 'round these parts."

"What kind of farm? This is all mountains, rocks, pine woods. What the hell do they farm up here? Besides, most of it's national park land."

She shrugged and swigged. "All I know is, three or four years back some corporation bought up a whole lot of land here and started farming it."

"What's this corporation called?"

"Oh...Allied Livestock and Farming. But I hear they use a lot of high tech stuff in giant greenhouses and under big plastic sheets."

I cut into the steak and speared some fries. "Allied Livestock and Farming, huh? Alfa. Do you know what crops they grow?"

She was looking at me curiously. Outside I heard some trucks pulling away. My guess was they were headed for the nearest town with a hospital. She shook her head. "I have no idea. Why are you so interested?"

I grinned at her. "Because I am a Viking raider, and I want to know if they have anything worth pillaging."

She sat back and pointed at me with her bottle. "You are trouble. You are big, bad trouble."

I stuffed the last piece of steak in my mouth and chewed. "You better believe it. Where is this place?"

"About three, four miles north-west of here, East of the Green Mountain. You take the North Spring Road, it'll lead you there eventually."

"Well, I won't be going tonight." I drained my beer and pulled a packet of Camels from my pocket. I lit up and inhaled deep. As I blew out I watched her through the smoke.

"Any other strangers been in town recently?"

"No."

"Where do you live, Blueberry?"

"Monday to Friday, right here."

"Good. Then how about you get us a bottle of tequila and we have a few shots before bed?"

Her cheeks flushed promisingly, she smiled and went to get the tequila.

I rose at five and went for a run. Blueberry had already gone back to her room. I got back at six, collected my kit bag from the trunk of the Zombie and took it up to my room. I showered and changed my clothes, strapped the Sig 226 under my arm and went down for breakfast at just before seven.

I had finished my bacon and eggs and I was on my second cup of coffee when the sheriff came in. Blueberry greeted him with all the enthusiasm of a tequila hangover and gave him a cup of coffee, which he brought over to my table and sat opposite me.

"Sheriff Mitch Hanafin. Mind if I join you?"

I leaned back in my chair and studied his face. He was overweight and had the small, hard eyes of a greedy man.

"What's on your mind, Sheriff?"

"Just wondering what a man like you is doing in a town like this."

"What kind of man am I?"

"That's what I am wondering, son."

I smiled. "Used to come up here when I was a kid, two weeks every year. Just spending a few days remembering old times."

"Does remembering old times include breaking men's arms and stabbing them in the neck?"

I pulled out my cigarettes and offered him one. He took it and I flipped my Zippo to light it. I let him see my hand was steady. Then I lit my own.

"Are you referring to the brawl that occurred here last night, out in the street?"

"You know I am."

I shook my head and gave a small laugh. "I had nothing to do with that, Sheriff. You surely can't think that I, on my own, could take on four men like that and remain unscathed." I showed him my hands. There were no bruises. If you break enough bricks with your fists, they don't bruise when you hit something as soft as a jaw.

He gave his head a twitch. "It is kind of hard to believe, I grant you. What happened?"

"I was chatting with Blueberry at the bar, and those boys went outside to settle an argument." I shrugged. "And that's all I know."

He knew I was lying, but he couldn't see where the lie was. So he just nodded and asked me, "You planning on staying in town much longer?"

"I plan to be gone by the day after tomorrow."

"Sounds like a plan to me. If you can make it sooner, so much the better. Strangers are not all that welcome here. Think of it as a closed community."

I watched him stand and sucked on my cigarette, squinting at him through the smoke. "I will keep that in mind, Sheriff. Thanks for the advice."

He offered me a thin, humorless smile. "Oh, it ain't advice." He hitched up his pants and left without paying for his coffee.

I looked at Blueberry. "He doesn't pay?"

She shook her head. "Some people don't pay."

"Who else doesn't pay?"

"Junkers and Maddox."

"Who are Junkers and Maddox?"

"Junkers is the foreman at the farm. Maddox is the manager."

"How often do they come in?"

She shrugged. "Junkers, maybe once a week on Saturday. Maddox, if he's in town."

I stood and took my plate and cup to the bar. "Point them out to me next time they're in."

I stepped out into the chill sunshine and climbed in my car. I lowered the windows to let the cool morning air in and headed slowly back toward the cabin, thinking about the Alfa farm, Junkers and Maddox, and Marni. Was it a coincidence that Alfa and Omega were at either extreme of the alphabet? Was it a coincidence that Marni had come here? Had she, by leaving that picture on the board in the kitchen, deliberately brought me here so I could see the farm?

I turned right at the junction and climbed the hill. As I was approaching the fork for the cabin, I pulled off the road and tucked the Zombie behind some trees, where it was hidden by the undergrowth. Then I climbed the rest of the way on foot.

When I arrived, the place was still and silent, aside from the birdsong and the odd rustle up in the canopy. I thought about searching the woods, but decided against it. As I had decided before—she would let me know when the time was right. I climbed the steps to the porch and found the door open, like last time. Inside, not much had changed. Some plates had been used and washed, and left to dry in the rack. Some embers were smoking in the fireplace, and there was a smell of soot. On the table there was a sketch pad, with a picture of a tree. I felt a single, hot thud in my chest. I knew the tree. It was the tree where she used to hide her treasures when we were kids.

It was a steep climb through dense woods and a thick undergrowth of ferns. At times I had to use my hands to haul myself up. The higher I went, the more the woodland was broken up by sudden outcrops of rocks and boulders that made the progress hard and slow. It had been over ten years, but I still remembered the way.

Finally, after almost an hour of climbing, I came out to a small plateau. To my left there was a deep, wooded gorge, and beyond it the high peak of Green Mountain. Ahead of me, the plateau fell away, among rocks and shrubs, and rose again to a bald, stone peak, about three hundred yards distant.

It was invisible until you got there, but there was a small cave—our Hole in the Wall—just beneath the peak. I felt a stab of something that might have been excitement, and might have been fear, that Marni would be there.

I pressed on.

It took me another twenty minutes of scrambling and stumbling, but eventually I got there and lowered myself down to the small hollow where the cave was. I pulled out my pencil flashlight and shone it inside. She wasn't there, but there were signs that she had been: some cushions, blankets, the cold remains of a small fire.

I turned. A little farther down the escarpment, shielded from view by rocks to the east and the wooded slopes on the north, west and south, was an ancient pinion pine, about forty feet high, with a thick tangle of foliage around its base. That was what had made it an ideal hiding place for her treasures.

I scrambled down, half sliding on my ass over the loose, dry earth, to the relatively flat area where the tree grew. Lying on my belly, I crawled in among the lower branches to the hollow she had cleared on the inside. I recognized the spot, close in among the roots, where she had dug a hole to store her things. I knelt there and dug with my fingers.

It was three inches below the surface. A simple piece of board which I levered up. And beneath it a hole, slightly more than a foot square and two feet deep. There were stones I recognized from when she was a kid, a couple of fossils, a rune I had carved for her on a pebble and strung with a leather thong, and a diary. The diary was new. That was why she had asked me to come here. For the diary.

I removed the Sig 232 from my boot and put it in the hole, with a spare magazine. Then I took out the diary, put back the board, and carefully covered it with dirt. After that, I slid out and made my way back toward the car.

The thought kept going over and over in my mind. She wanted me to find the diary. Not her, the diary.

Why?

Seven

IT WAS FOUR IN THE afternoon by the time I got back to the diner in Turret. The tables were empty and stood in gloomy shadows among dusty beams of light from the windows. Blueberry seemed to have recovered from her hangover, and draped herself around me as I walked in. I gave her a kiss and said, "How about you fix me a hamburger and a very cold beer?"

She rolled her eyes and pranced into the kitchen. I sat at the bar and she called out, "You gonna tell me what you're doing here?"

"No."

"How about if I tell you about the two guys who were askin' about you?"

She poked her head out of the kitchen door, smiling. I shook my head. "Still no."

"You tell me, I tell you."

I sighed. "I'll tell you this much. Those men are killers. If they think you know anything of what I know, they will torture you and kill you. Your smart move is to tell me who they are and where they are staying. When they come around, act like you don't know me. And never again try to find out why I am here."

She became serious and went back in the kitchen. A couple of minutes later she put a giant burger in front of me and cracked me an ice cold beer.

"They were city types. Designer survival clothes, Timberland boots, Armani hunting hats. You know the type?"

I nodded.

"They had a Wrangler Unlimited. Said they were here for the hunting, and had I seen their pal."

"What did you tell them?"

"I said I didn't know. I said we get a few people coming through summer and autumn. So he described you. Said your name was Lacklan, you were driving a souped-up Mustang and you might be with your wife."

"What did you say?"

"I said someone like that had rolled through couple of days ago, but they'd moved on."

"You shouldn't have done that. You should have told them I was here."

"You're welcome."

"I'm serious, Blueberry. These men are dangerous. You put your life at risk." She went a little pale. "When they come back, I want you to call them over, ask them if I am their buddy. You understand?"

She looked a bit sick. "What will they do to you?"

"Nothing. I'm going to kill them."

"*Jesus, Lacklan!* What the fuck?"

"Where are they staying?"

"They said they were in Salida, but they wanted to know if I had any rooms. I said I was booked up at the moment. They said they'd be back this evening, and maybe I'd have room for them then. They said it kind of menacing. We've got a couple of cabins up the road, but I didn't want to tell them..."

I thought for a moment. "Where do you live?"

"I told you..."

"No, your real home. Where do you go on the weekend?"

"Salida, with my folks."

"When these men come back, give them one of the cabins. If they want to eat, serve them dinner. Then go. Go home. By tomorrow they'll be gone. Now, show me the cabin you're going to give them."

After I'd looked at the cabin I went up to my room to have a shower and read the diary I had recovered from the tree. It wasn't current. It was from a couple of years after she had graduated, while she was doing her doctoral thesis. A lot of it was just reflections about her work and comments about colleagues. But, as I read through the pages, I also noticed how her earlier naïve, volatile concern about the environment as a whole gradually began to take shape as a focused, well-informed passion. And also how she gradually became more aware of her father and how he had blazed the trail for her. Even when we were kids, she had held him on a pedestal, though she had barely known him. He had inspired her and represented everything that was good and noble.

It was ironic that as her father had been her inspiration and she had devoted her life to following him, so mine had represented for me everything that was the worst in humanity, and I had devoted my life to distancing myself from him. My father had killed hers, and now I was fighting to save her life, so that her father's spirit and work could live on.

I slept for an hour, dressed, and went down at seven, as darkness was drawing in. There were a couple of tables occupied and I could hear more trucks arriving outside. The place was starting to fill up. Some of the the men at the tables glanced over as I came in, but other than that they ignored me, which suited me fine. Blueberry was cooking. I went behind the bar, took a beer from the fridge and threw some coins on the cash register. I leaned in the kitchen and told Blueberry to make me a steak. Then I went to sit in the farthest corner, to wait for the hunters from Salida.

I didn't have to wait long. They rolled in at just before eight, and they were exactly how she had described them. Only, to me, as well as being city types with designer hunting gear, they had professional killer written all over them. I knew the type well. They'd done a few years in the military, then graduated to mercenaries in Africa, burning villages and killing women and children. Then they got cushy jobs with a 'security agency' contracting for the CIA on jobs that were too dirty even for spooks. They were noisy and aggressive, and believed themselves above the law. They were probably right. Depends whose law.

I studied them, how they moved, where their weaknesses were. The smaller, leaner one sat at a table. He had sallow skin and black hair. He was hard and flexible. You could tell he worked out a lot. He was laughing as his pal leaned on the bar, shouting to Blueberry.

"Hey! Sweet cheeks! Your favorite hunters are back. Tell me you got a room for us!"

He was big. Six-four at least. He had big shoulders and strong arms and legs. But he also had a big belly. He was greedy and relied too much on his muscular strength. He was going bald and had a rim of sandy hair from ear to ear across the back of his head.

Blueberry came out of the kitchen carrying two plates of food. Her cheeks were flushed, either from cooking or from fear. She was smiling breathlessly.

"Hey guys! I'll do better than that!" She walked past the big guy toward a table with four farmers sitting at it, talking over her shoulder as she went. "I found your friend!"

The two men looked at each other and then back at her. The big guy said, "No kidding. Where is he?"

She put down the plates in front of the farm boys, said, "Enjoy your meal," then turned and beamed at me across the room.

"Why, he's right there! I'm surprised you ain't seen him already!"

They turned to look at me with dangerous leers on their faces. Blueberry hurried back into the kitchen as the big guy said, "Well, hello there, Lacklan. I hadn't seen you, hiding there in the corner." His friend stood and they approached the table. "Mind if we join you?"

They pulled out the chairs and sat. The sallow one spoke for the first time.

"I'm Smith, this is Jones. We've been looking for you."

Smith and Jones, cute. "How did you find me?"

Jones smiled all over his big face. "Well, we have our ways, Lacklan. Have you found Marni?"

I studied his face a moment, then Smith's, wondering which was in charge and which was most dangerous. "Who do you work for?"

Smith said, "You don't seem to understand the game, Lacklan. We ask, you answer."

Blueberry emerged from the kitchen with my steak. She looked real scared. She put it in front of me and I asked her what time it was. She looked at her watch. "Eight fifteen."

I nodded. She knew what it meant. She had forty-five minutes. Then she had to leave. She turned to Jones and handed him a key. "I got you a swell little cabin, right on the cross roads. Y'all gonna be real cozy there."

He leered at her. "Well thank you, sweet cheeks. You going to join us there for a party later?"

She giggled hysterically and fled back to the kitchen. I cut into the steak and stuffed a piece in my mouth. I spoke as I chewed.

"If you want information from me, you better be prepared to give me something in return."

Jones said, "Like what?"

"I want money, and I want information."

He was frowning. Clearly, he had not expected this. "How much money?"

I laughed. "Well, guys. They say silence is golden. How much do *you* think silence is worth?"

I cut at the steak again and watched the blood ooze onto the plate. They were staring. Smith said, "We were not told to negotiate. We were told to find you and find the girl."

I chewed, tasting the blood, and took my time drinking from the bottle. I sighed as I put it down. "That's the problem with employing assholes like you guys. Because things just got complicated for you, and you haven't the intelligence to adapt. See? The girl has the information that your boss does not want the media to get hold of. I know where the girl is. So you think, 'get Lacklan, get the girl.' Simple. Only now Lacklan has gone and complicated things. Because he's hidden the girl *and* he has acquired the information. This means your boss' problem has increased exponentially. Now *two* people have the information, and two people can release it to the media, but you only know where one of those people is. Kill me, and you fuck up *everything*. The whole fucking thing explodes in your faces."

They were staring at each other. They looked annoyed, even a little offended. This was not what they were told to expect. I finished my steak and peeled a fresh pack of Camels, leaning back in my chair. I fished one out and took my time lighting it.

"What is the solution to this problem, gentlemen? It's simple. It is the solution to all problems. Money. For the right money, you get the girl, and my guarantee of silence. But I need something else."

Smith's frown deepened. "What else?"

"I need you to give Maddox a message from me."

"What?"

I smiled. It was too easy. "Tell him I know what he's doing at the farm. My silence won't come cheap."

Jones looked pissed. He made to stand. "Come on. We need to call him." He looked at me. "Where are you staying?"

"Here."

"How did you know about Maddox?"

I was about to tell him I hadn't, just to watch him squirm. Instead I said, "The girl. She knows a damn sight more than you think. And now, so do I."

They stood and left. I looked at my watch. It was twenty to nine. I gave it ten minutes, then stood and pulled my Sig from under my arm. I walked to the bar and let off a round into the ceiling. Blueberry screamed and everybody turned to look at me.

"All right, gentlemen, nothing to be alarmed about. It is Wednesday, early closing. Please drink up and make your way home. Now. Drive careful."

Within five minutes the bar was empty and the parking lot was full of reversing trucks and beams from headlamps like crazy lighthouses in the dark. Blueberry gave me a long, lingering kiss on the porch as the last of the cars pulled away. "I knew you were trouble. You are one scary son of a bitch. Please be careful."

I shook my head. "No."

She left.

Eight

I LOCKED UP AND SLIPPED out the kitchen door in back. The moon had not risen yet over the peaks to the east, and the sky was dark. Though the horizon was pale and I could hear coyotes baying in the distance. I took a moment to screw the silencer onto the Sig and slipped it into my waistband. Then I sprinted silently toward the cluster of trees that surrounded the crossroads. There I dropped on my belly and fitted the night vision goggles over my eyes. There wasn't a lot to see. The cabin was dark except for one window with a dim light in it at the front of the house.

I knew they hadn't called Maddox because there was no cell reception up here, and I had taken the precaution of cutting their phone lines. So I knew I wasn't going to get any unwelcome visitors. When I was satisfied there was nobody watching, I ran the remaining thirty yards to the back of the house. There were no lights in the kitchen, and the spare key was where I had left it, under a rock by the door. I let myself in and stood listening.

They were watching TV in the living room. I pulled the Sig from my belt. My plan was to take out Smith with a double tap, neutralize Jones and interrogate him. I moved down the short passage, braced myself outside the door and moved to kick it in, holding the Sig out in front of me in both hands.

Then everything went wrong at the same time. A loud voice boomed, "I'm famished. You want something to eat?" At the same time, the door wrenched open and my foot kicked empty air. I over-balanced and stumbled forward. For a fraction of a second I saw Jones, a couple of feet away, gawping at me. Past him, sitting in an armchair, Smith was staring in astonishment.

I tried to swing the weapon around toward Jones, but his massive fist smashed into my face and sent me staggering back against the wall, dazed and stunned, with the room spinning and rocking underneath me. Next thing he had me by the scruff of my neck and was dragging me to my feet. I swung the Sig toward his belly but he grabbed my wrist, bellowing at Smith to come help him.

His mistake was not to finish me immediately. He gave me those precious seconds for the adrenaline to kick in. And by then it was too late. He had my right wrist and my throat in his massive hands. He thought he had enough time for Smith to come and help him. He didn't. I pulled myself in close with my right arm and slammed my left fist into his floating ribs. He was tough and I knew he wouldn't let go. But all I wanted was for him to loosen his grip on my wrist. He did. I angled the automatic down and put two slugs into his leg. He screamed and fell.

Smith was behind him. He lashed out with his foot and he was a lot faster than I had expected. He knocked the gun from my hand and as he landed, he pounded my belly with four powerful punches that almost knocked the wind out of me. His fifth was with his fingertips and aimed at my throat. It would have killed me.

I dodged left so the blow flashed over my right shoulder, and slammed the heel of my hand into his chin. He staggered back two steps and hit the door frame. Jones was still sobbing on the floor. Smith was dazed and I saw his next move coming. Tae Kwon Do was his style, and as I came at him he lunged into a front kick which would have ruptured my liver. Instead I lifted my knee to deflect the blow, and as I did so I slipped the fighting knife from my boot. He landed from the kick already drawing back his fist, but by that time the six-inch, double-edged blade was already deep in his heart. He quivered and spasmed, and blood gurgled from his mouth. I let him slip off the blade to slump on the floor and turned to look at Jones.

"You fucked up every step of the way, Mr. Jones."

He was sobbing. I hunkered down beside him.

"I can stop the bleeding and get you to a doctor in Salida in about twenty minutes. You might lose the leg, you might not. But if I don't get you there, you will bleed out in about ten to fifteen. You going to talk to me?"

He nodded. "Please help me."

"How did you find me?"

"A tracker."

"Where?"

"In your kit bag."

"How?"

"Your dad's man, Ben."

"What is Maddox doing?"

"I don't know, man. It's nothing to do with us. We were just sent to get the girl."

"Who by?"

"Maddox."

"So Maddox is part of Omega?"

"Yeah, I thought you knew that! Come on man, I'm dying here!"

"Who is Maddox's boss?"

"*I don't know!* We are just hired muscle, man!"

I nodded and stood. I went into the living room where the TV was playing a repeat of an ancient sitcom. Smith's Glock was on the coffee table. I picked it up with my handkerchief and carried it over to where Smith was lying. I fitted it into his right hand and placed his finger on the trigger. Jones was staring at me. I said, "Wrong answer," and shot him through the heart.

I dug out my two 9mm slugs from his leg and put them in my pocket. I was pretty sure they wouldn't have a CSI team running ballistics on these two, but it pays to be careful. I didn't know if Sheriff Hanafin was Maddox's man or not. But if he wasn't, all he was going to see was the ugly result of a brawl between two hunters. He would investigate no further.

If he was Maddox's man, then it made no difference. He'd know who'd done it, ballistics or not. And if he was Maddox's man, I wanted him to know.

I took the keys to the Jeep, made my way back to the diner and climbed the stairs to my room. I emptied out my kit bag on the bed and went through my clothes and my weapons one by one. I didn't find the tracking device. I opened the Velcro flaps and pulled out the arrows. It was in the third arrow pocket - a small disk stuck to the canvas.

I sat looking at it a while, wondering if only Smith and Jones had been receiving its signal or whether it was transmitting to somebody else as well. There was no way of being sure, but there was an at least even chance whoever was running the Armani Hunters, whoever had instructed Ben to place the transmitter in my bag, was also receiving the signal.

I lit a cigarette and sat thinking about my next move. For a moment I had the impulse to go to the cabin and grab Marni. I knew I could do it, and I knew she'd be there. But I dismissed the idea. She didn't want me to find her yet. She wanted me to go after the Farm and Maddox. That much was clear to me now, and if that was what she wanted, she must have her reasons.

I took a spare magazine for the Sig, cleaned my knife, put it back in my boot, and broke off a chunk of C4. I also put an M5 detonator in my pocket. The night-vision goggles were still around my neck. I knew what I had to do, and I knew where to do it.

I went back out and found Jones and Smith's Jeep. The moon, in its last waxing, was just rising over the mountains. I climbed in to the truck, fired up the big V6 and drove half a mile out of town along North Spring Road. There was a derelict shack out there that was going to serve my purpose. I didn't try to be silent or keep hidden. If anyone was watching or listening, I wanted them to know where I was going.

I found the place and came off the road, bumped up the track for a hundred yards, and finally came to a stop outside the old semi-ruin. The door was unlocked and I went inside. Thin moonlight was filtering in through the dirty glass in the windows. I pulled out my pencil flashlight and played the beam around the room. There wasn't much there, save a pot-bellied stove and a rocking chair.

I returned to the door and wedged it closed. Using my knife, I levered up one of the floorboards and placed the C4 beneath it, with the tracking device tucked into it. I stabbed in the detonator, connected it to the handle of the door and replaced the floorboard. The next person to open that door would bring the house down.

I let myself out through the bedroom window and returned to the Jeep. I was smiling. As I climbed behind the wheel, I thought of Marni, of her goodness. I wondered for a moment, had I lost my humanity? I decided I hadn't, but like I said, I was working on it.

Nine

I BUMPED AND GROUND my way back down the track and turned north at the end. Now I left the headlamps off and relied on the rising moon to find my way. There was no black-top to reflect the light. I had to follow the ghostly ribbon of pale earth that lay between the shrubs and sparse woodland.

I drove slowly, keeping my eyes focused ahead and to the left, where Blueberry had said the farm would be. After three or four minutes the road turned west and all I could see ahead was the dark forms of the trees looming at the sides of the road, and the black silhouette of the mountains ahead. I kept going for another five minutes, crawling at ten or fifteen MPH, scanning for any sign of cultivation, lights, anything that might suggest a farm.

I didn't see anything until the road turned north again after about a mile. Then I began to make out what looked like tall fenceposts. I slowed and pulled over. They were barely visible, but they were there, about thirty feet back from the road. I killed the engine and jumped down. On closer inspection I saw that the posts, about a foot square and seven feet high, had a wire mesh strung across them, and a little experimentation with my knife showed the mesh was electrically charged.

I returned to the Jeep and tucked it behind some trees on the far side of the road, then fitted the night vision goggles and returned at a lope to the fence. There I lay in the dry grass, twenty feet back, and waited. They came after ten minutes, black silhouettes against an eerie green backlight, driving an open top Wrangler. There were two of them and they were armed with automatic rifles. They parked with their headlamps on full beam aimed at the spot where I had held the knife against the wires with my boot and walked over to examine it. One of the two guys hunkered down to look at the wires. His eyes shone green where the headlamps reflected off them. I heard him say, "Probably just a coyote, or a fuckin' jackrabbit. The mesh ain't busted."

The other muttered something and I saw green mist rise from his mouth where he had a cigarette dangling. They withdrew, climbed back in the Wrangler and drove away. I gave them five minutes and began to walk along the edge of the fence, taking my time, looking for some place where it could be breached.

I didn't find one, but after a while I began to see light filtering up from behind a line of trees, maybe a quarter of a mile away. I figured that must be the main building of the farm. I walked for another ten minutes and up ahead, I started to make out a small construction. It was maybe thirty or forty yards away and there was a faint luminescence coming off it. I dropped on my belly and began to crawl. At fifteen yards, I could see that it was a guard's hut, and it was attached to a large, metal gate.

I thought about taking out the guard and going in that way, but it presented too many obstacles, so I turned back the way I had come. The impression I had was that they didn't want visitors, but neither did they really expect them. The fence was less of an obstacle than a deterrent. Most of the people in the neighborhood worked here anyway, according to Blueberry. It seemed to me they just wanted to put off any nosey hikers or teens from coming in and snooping.

I got back to the Jeep, climbed in and drove it slowly to within an inch of the nearest post. Then I climbed on the hood and vaulted over the fence into the grounds of the farm. Getting out again would not be a problem, as long as I didn't get caught.

I set off at a rifleman's run, ten paces walking, ten paces running, toward a large hill about a quarter of a mile away. Behind it I could see the faint glow I had seen earlier. Every now and then I would catch a waft of sound on the breeze, like heavy trucks moving, or heavy machinery. A couple of times I dropped to the ground because I thought I heard a Jeep, but I managed to reach the bottom of the hill without being seen.

By now the glow behind the hill was intense, and the sound of machinery was distinct and clear. There were diesel engines at work there. I ran the forty yards to the top and dropped on my belly to crawl the last few feet to the rim.

I don't know what I had expected to see, but it was not what I saw. What I saw was a military installation. It was vast. At a guess I figured it was two or three hundred yards long, and about the same across, which put it in the region of five to seven hectares. It was surrounded by a double barbed wire fence, with eight towers—one at each corner and one in the middle of each fence. I could see men with automatic weapons and dogs patrolling the space between the fences, and two armed guards in each of the towers. They appeared to be wearing military fatigues.

In the center of the square there were prefabricated structures, two stories high and painted a dull green color, standing at right angles to each other, forming smaller squares, perhaps forty yards across. These areas were covered in white plastic sheets. The whole thing was floodlit as bright as day, but apart from the guards on the perimeter fence, I saw practically no people.

The far north end of the enclosure was at the foot of a cliff, where the ground rose suddenly toward one of the mountain peaks. There, annexed to the camp, was a vast hangar, painted the same ugly sage green as the huts. It was hard to estimate its size from that distance, but it was at least thirty to forty yards across and the height of an apartment block. As I watched, I heard an engine from the southwestern side. When I looked, I saw a couple of guards opening a gate to allow a truck to come in. It was loaded with what looked like sunflowers. I heard the gears grind and it made its way through the compound, and eventually through the doors of the hangar.

I stared past the gates into the shadows beyond. The glare from the installation below made it hard to see, but as I shielded my eyes I gradually became aware, in the moonlight, that there were acres of fields, stretching as far as the eye could see. Fields of what, in that poor visibility, looked like sunflowers.

I stayed another half hour, watching, and in that time another three trucks rolled in, each loaded with sunflowers.

I slid back down the hill and set off toward the outer fence at a steady jog. In the strange, turquoise light of the moon, it took me ten minutes to cover the distance back to the Jeep. As I approached the fencepost, I accelerated to a sprint, then jumped. The only thing I had to be careful of was to touch the fence only with the soles of my boots. It was two steps, and then grab the top of the post with my hands. I levered myself up and jumped down onto the hood of the Jeep.

I was certain I had set off an alarm, but by the time they got there I would be long gone. Another damn coyote.

As I drove away I poked a Camel in my mouth, flipped my Zippo and leaned in to the flame, thinking about sunflowers. What the hell would make anybody guard sunflowers with soldiers and barbed wire? What did sunflowers have that was so valuable?

But even as I was thinking, crawling my way along the luminous dust path, I knew it was not just the sunflowers. Because you could get millions of tons of sunflowers anywhere you liked where there was sun. Which meant that the sunflowers they were growing here were special in some way. So the question was, what made these sunflowers special?

A: they were genetically modified in some way, or B: they processed them in some way in the complex or in the hangar, or both. That might make sense the complex was more heavily guarded than the fields.

So now the question became, what were they doing to the sunflowers in the complex and in the hangar? And as far as I could tell, there was only one way to find out.

I left the Jeep outside Smith and Jones' cabin and walked back to the diner. I let myself in and took a bottle of Irish from behind the bar. I sat at a table with it and smoked and drank and thought. Maddox and his farm were part of Omega, but only part. I knew the operation was bigger, and Maddox had bosses above him. I had to use him to get to them.

They had sent men with guns after me and Marni. Now I would take blood, fire and destruction to them.

I didn't sleep. Eventually I went upstairs and lay on the bed, waiting for morning. I saw the translucent light of the moon change through my open window to the grim, gray light of dawn. No trucks rolled in at six for early breakfast. At seven, I went down and made coffee and toast and took it out on the porch to wait. At eight, Blueberry arrived in her Toyota. She climbed out and stood looking at me. She looked scared.

"What did you do, Lacklan?"

I raised my cup. "I made coffee."

She climbed the steps, went inside, and started setting up shop.

At half past eight, the explosion tore through the morning, scattered birds screaming into the sky, made the windows rattle, sent splintered wood, shards of glass and bits of human body two hundred feet up into the air, to rain down on the town from a mushroom cloud of dust and smoke that would linger over Turret like a ghost for the rest of the day.

Blueberry came rushing out into the street to stare up at the sky. Then she stared at me. I was smiling. The war had begun. I am good at war. War is what I do best.

Ten

THE SHERIFF ARRIVED an hour later with two deputies. Blueberry had a shed around back and I had asked her to let me put the Zombie in there, to keep her out of sight and charge her up. I was coming back from doing that when I saw the sheriff's Ford pick-up speed toward the smoldering remains of the booby-trapped cabin.

I climbed the steps to the porch and went inside. It was dark after the glare of the morning sun. Blueberry was sitting on a stool at the bar with a beam of dusty light illuminating her face. She didn't look happy.

"Who are you? Why are you here?"

"It's best you don't know." I went behind the counter and poured myself a coffee. "Things are going to get pretty ugly in the next couple of days. You'd be best staying at home."

"That's not how we do things 'round here. You don't run away just coz things get tough."

I carried my coffee to the window and stood looking out. They'd be coming soon. She spoke behind me. She sounded mad, resentful.

"My parents opened this business. Who's going to compensate them for the money they're going to lose?"

I answered without turning. "I'm sorry about that. I'll see what I can do."

"That's how it is with you, huh? Walk in, use people, kill people, destroy things... 'Sorry about that,' and walk away..."

"I guess so." I turned to face her. "I can't explain to you what's going on, Blueberry. All I can tell you is that these are very dangerous people. If you stay, your life is at risk, and I don't want you to get hurt."

She stared at me, hard. Outside, I heard the Sheriff's truck and knew he was going to Smith and Jones' cabin. Her eyes shifted over my shoulder and then back to my face.

"You're an asshole," she said simply and went into the kitchen. I took my coffee outside and sat on the porch to watch the activity at the deceased duo's dwelling.

After ten minutes, the Sheriff came out and talked on the radio. I figured he was calling for a meat wagon. After a moment he hung up, saw me and walked over with the measured steps of a genuine Wyatt Earp, hitching up his trousers over his belly as he went.

I watched him climb the steps and stand looking down at me.

"Good morning, Sheriff. Have some coffee?"

"You still here, huh?"

"I find the air stimulating."

"You have anything to do with any of this?"

"Any of what, Sheriff? Are you here about the explosion up the road? That fair shook the windows." I smiled amiably.

He narrowed his eyes in a way he thought was menacing and nodded. "So far we found four legs and three hands. So at least two men were killed by that explosion..."

"That seems arithmetically sound."

"Don't get smart with me, son."

"Were they playing with explosives? Perhaps it was a terror-ist cell. This could be a career-defining moment for you, Sher-iff."

He pointed over at the cabin. "Two fellers in that cabin came here looking for you. This morning they show up dead."

I shook my head. "That was a mistake. Blueberry thought it was me they were looking for, but it turned out to be some-body else." I made a face like I was concerned. "How did they die?"

He pointed a sausage-finger at me. "I have my eye on you, Walker. You better watch your step."

I smiled. "Only malefactors fear the eye of the law, Sheriff. The righteous need never hide from it. Amen."

He pushed into the diner and the door banged behind him. I sipped my coffee and ran over things in my mind again. If I was right, Maddox would be there within the hour.

As it was, he was there within the half hour. He arrived in a black limo with tinted windows. His driver opened the back door for him and he stepped out, buttoning his Italian jacket. He glanced at me, climbed the stairs and pushed into the diner with his driver behind him. I knew what was coming next, and I was right. Ten minutes later, the driver stepped out again. He was big, with a barrel chest and a thick neck. He stood in front of me like a statue of the Buddha on a bad hair day and said, "Mr. Maddox wants to see you."

I blinked at him a few times to show I was a little confused. "OK..."

He frowned. "Inside."

"No, see, I'm out here. If he wants to see me, he's going to have to come outside."

His big face hardened. "He wants to see you *inside*."

I watched him but I didn't answer. The door opened and the sheriff leaned out. "Walker. Get your ass in here. Mr. Maddox wants to talk to you."

I shifted my gaze from the gorilla to the sheriff. "No."

I heard a chair scrape inside and angry feet striding across the wooden floor. Maddox pushed past the sheriff. He stood next to his driver and squinted down at me, somewhere between being mad and being curious.

"You are playing a very stupid game, Walker." I frowned down at my coffee. He went on. "I know why you are here, and you better believe me when I tell you, it is in your best interest to cooperate with me, because neither you nor that bitch have a chance in hell of getting away with this."

I looked up. "With what, Maddox?"

The sheriff snarled, "That's *Mr*. Maddox to you, Walker!"

I stood and stepped real close to Maddox. "Let me make a couple of things clear to you, Maddox. First, I am not playing. Whatever reason I am here, is real. It is no game. Second, I have no idea in what ways you think we can cooperate, but threatening me is not the way to get my cooperation. Threats make me kind of crazy. And third, I don't know what *bitch* you're referring to. As far as I am aware, your wife is still in bed, where I left her."

The big gorilla didn't so much telegraph the punch as give a month's notice that it was coming. It was easy to block and get right inside his guard, where I slammed my fist down hard onto his belly, just bellow his solar plexus. The combined weight of the punch and his gut dragged down his diaphragm, winded him and drained all the blood from his head. He made a noise like a car with a dying battery and collapsed on the decking.

The sheriff fumbled for his .38. I gave him the dead eye and spoke quietly. "You un-holster that, Sheriff, you better kill me."

You could see the math going on in his brain. Two at the shack, two in the cabin, three maimed and one dead the night before. His odds didn't look so great. Maddox put a hand on the sheriff's arm. The sheriff looked relieved.

"All right, Mitch, let's not escalate this." He sighed. "Walker, all I want to do is talk to you…"

"So talk. I'm right here and I'm listening. What do you want?"

"You know what I want. I want the girl."

I shrugged. "What girl?"

He was getting antsy again. "You know what girl, Walker! And you know that I know! I can make this worth your while!"

I smiled in a way that was amiable. "Gee, Sheriff, I honestly think you have me confused with somebody else."

His face flushed and made him look like a beetroot in an Armani suit. "I am warning you, Walker. You may be good at what you do, but you are taking on more than you understand. I want your cooperation to find this slut, but if I can't get it, your life isn't worth a damn! I will hunt you both down and I will kill you both."

I looked at the sheriff. "I am going to give you a chance, Sheriff. I have been attacked, and I have just been threatened with death. Are you going to arrest this man?"

Sheriff Hanafin sneered. "Get real, Walker."

I looked back at Maddox. "So we are operating outside the law?"

He shook his head. "A different law, Walker. My law."

The driver was staggering to his feet, leaning on the handrail. He turned to me and his chin and his shirt were smeared with vomit.

I said, "Friend, get out of here, because next time we meet I will kill you." I turned back to the Sheriff. "For you and this clown, there is no escape, Sheriff. Before thirty-six hours are up, you'll both be dead."

I saw fear in their eyes.

Maddox started to talk. "You are making a big mistake..."

I silenced him. "I am going to bring destruction and devastation to you, Maddox, on a scale you can't imagine. And then, when you see the ruins of everything you have done around you, I will kill you."

They fumbled down the steps. Maddox and his driver clambered into their limo, and the sheriff went at a shambling run across the dirt road toward his pick-up. The lines were drawn. Now I had to prepare. I turned to go inside. Blueberry was standing in the doorway, watching me.

"You're out of your mind," she said.

I said, "Go home."

Eleven

I WATCHED THE ME, THE ambulance and the sheriff drive off in a convoy. It had never been his intention to arrest me. If it had been, he'd have deputized a dozen of Maddox's men and taken me in, dead or alive. Besides, he had no hard evidence against me that would stand up in a court of law. No, the sheriff had been told to beat it and let Maddox take care of things.

When they'd gone, I had a bite to eat and told Blueberry to get together some bread and cheese. I added that to my kit bag. I figured the farm was about one and a half or two miles away as the crow flies. The outlying fields, which were what interested me right then, might be a bit closer than that. The terrain was rough and hilly, so I was going to allow myself a couple of hours to get there.

At two o'clock, I slung my bag over my shoulder and stepped out onto the porch. Blueberry came out after me.

"Lacklan, just get in your car and go."

"I can't do that."

"You're really crazy about her, huh?"

I shook my head. "That isn't an option."

"She's a lucky girl."

"Not really."

"You know you're going to get killed, don't you?"

"It's possible."

"I'll miss you."

I gave her a kiss. "I don't want to find you here when I get back. Go home."

She looked me in the eye. "I told you. That's not how we do things in these parts."

I turned and walked away. I didn't follow the road. I went to the back of the diner and headed northeast, sticking to the woodland and keeping below the high ground. It was warm and the going was heavy and slow. There were lots of hills and the land was covered in loose rocks, stones and sand. After an hour, I crested a high escarpment with large boulders at the top. I knew from this point the ground gradually sloped away toward the farm.

I clambered to the top of the highest boulder and lay on my belly, looking toward where I knew the farm was. Despite its size, it took me a while to make out the hangar. The dirty sage green was a perfect match for the environment it was in. Once I had it, I began to make out the enclosure, and then the fields to the west. I adjusted my binoculars and had a closer look. The area they covered was vast. Several hectares. And the trucks were still on their non-stop routine, going to the fields, collecting the plants and delivering them to the hangar. From where I was lying, about a mile distant, it was hard to be sure, but the operation seemed to be mainly mechanized. As I had noticed the night before, there didn't seem to be many people involved.

I ate a piece of bread and some cheese and kept going, bearing west toward the fields that lay furthest from the enclosure. Now the going was slower and more difficult, because as I drew closer, the risk of being seen was proportionally greater. The need to stay low among the sparse trees was greater with every hundred paces I took.

Finally, after another hour, as the sun was beginning to slip from the zenith, I scrambled to the top of a wooded slope and peered over the edge. I was ten or twelve paces from the electrified fence, and immediately beyond it was a dense field of fifteen foot sunflowers. They were arranged in rows, each about forty-five to fifty feet across, separated by dirt tracks about the width of a truck. A little distance away, I could hear the grinding of a diesel engine in low gear.

But there was another sound too, a buzzing that could have been bees or cicadas, but wasn't. It was coming from in among the sunflowers, and as I peered closer I realized that the plants were swarming with small, golden beetles. I listened a little longer and realized that the sound of the diesel engine was not moving. Whatever it was doing, it was doing it in one place.

I slipped over the top of the hill, ran and leapt for the top of the nearest post, using the rubber soles of my boots to keep me away from the electrified wires. I pulled myself up, rolled over and landed on my feet on the other side. I knew I had a couple of minutes at best before guards showed up to check the fence. I sprinted down the path between the sunflower plantations, toward the sound of the truck. There was a T-junction up ahead and the noise was coming from the left branch.

I skidded around and stopped. It looked like a seven-ton open truck with a mechanical arm. The arm was reaching out and ripping up 'handfuls' of plants, then dumping them in the back of the vehicle. There was a guy in a yellow safety helmet with his back to me, holding a wireless controller and smoking a cigarette. I glanced up at the cab. There was nobody else in it. He was on his own.

I didn't think. I pulled the knife from my boot and I was on him in two silent strides. In the movies, you always see them grab the guy's forehead and cut from left to right, dragging the blade across the throat. That's the wrong way. You grip the mouth and nose with your left hand, and you push the knife in on the right side of the neck. You push in hard and slice out, severing the jugular and the trachea, and you virtually decapitate him at the same time. He loses consciousness and bleeds out in a matter of seconds. That's what this guy did.

I took his helmet and his wireless controller. I used it to make the mechanical arm pick him up and dump him in the field among the sunflowers and the bugs. The truck looked just about full so I clambered in the cab and drove off in the direction of the compound, with my kit bag on the seat beside me. As I moved along, a Jeep sped past in the opposite direction with two armed guards in it. I smiled to myself. Another damned coyote.

It was a half-mile drive. The dirt tracks were on a grid system, so it was pretty simple. Here and there I saw trucks ripping up flowers and dumping them in their containers at the back. In other parts I saw machines that seemed to be plowing and planting at the same time.

Eventually, I came to the enclosure. I figured the double barbed-wire fence was about fifteen feet high, topped with a coil of razor wire. I pulled up at a big gate with a hut in front. There were two guards armed with automatic weapons. They were wearing military fatigues and they had a military look and feel about them. You develop an instinct over time, and these guys were not paramilitary. I was prepared to lay money that they were the real thing.

One of them squinted in at me and said, "Where's Jim? This is Jim's truck."

I shrugged like I didn't give a damn. "He got sick. I was sent to replace him."

"Why weren't we notified?"

I gave him a look that told him I didn't need his problems. "Ask someone who gives a fuck, pal. I do what I'm told."

He opened the gate and I watched him in the mirror to see what he did. He looked at me disappear for a bit, then went to talk to his pal. He didn't get on the radio, and that was a good thing.

As I drove on toward the hangar, I tried to get a look at the green huts and see what was under the plastic sheets, but there wasn't much to see, just tinted windows and a bit of foliage. I wound on past the huts and crossed a large esplanade where the vast doors of the hangar yawned open into a dark, impenetrable interior.

I slowed and moved in at a crawl. I saw a guy ahead beckoning me forward with his hands and glancing to the side occasionally. Then he told me to halt and gave me the thumbs up.

I didn't know if I was supposed to stay in the cab or not. I killed the engine and he turned and walked away. I grabbed my bag, opened the cab door and jumped out.

As I stood and watched, I realized that I was not in a warehouse. I was in a processing plant. My truck was being unloaded by another mechanical arm which was dumping the sunflower plants onto a conveyor belt, which in turn was carrying them towards a kind of vast grinding machine, like a giant micer. From the other end, a tube carried the resulting pulp deeper into the hangar, where it seemed to be mixed with other ingredients from hoppers overhead. That was what I could see at a glance. There were practically no people here, but I knew if I stood staring I was bound to attract somebody's attention. So I moved on. Besides, I needed to get rid of my kit bag somewhere.

And as I wondered what to do next, I saw a guy in a white lab coat with a clipboard striding toward me. He was frowning. I bent my knees a couple of times, spat on the floor and went and stood in the doorway to light a cigarette.

"Hey, you!"

I turned and gave him a 'fuck you' look.

He said, "What the hell do you think you're doing? Get in your cab and get this damn truck out of here!"

A foreman. You got to love a foreman. I gave him a once-over and said, "It ain't empty yet."

"What the hell are you talking about?"

I looked conciliatory and said, "C'mere. Have a look."

I beckoned him over to the back of the truck, had a quick look around, saw nobody was looking and smashed his head against the container. I put on his coat and hauled him onto the conveyor, then picked up his clipboard and slung my bag in the corner under the belt. As I strolled back the way he had come, I saw his foot disappearing into the grinder, to be masticated by the jaws of impermanence.

I looked at the paper on the clipboard. It didn't make a lot of sense. Some figures were in tons, which I assumed referred to the sunflowers. Other figures referred to units and lots, but of what was impossible to tell.

A sudden thought made me stop in my tracks and I walked back toward the area where the gigantic flowers were being loaded onto the conveyor belt. I went up close and peered at the plants. As in the field, they were swarming with the small, golden bugs. Whatever the pulp was for, it was not just sunflower pulp. It was sunflower and bug pulp.

I walked on. The guy who had guided me in appeared from across the floor, coming at a run. Another truck was approaching outside.

"Where the fuck is Jim? Get this fuckin' truck outa here! *Jim!* Where the fuck is Jim? *Jim!*"

I strolled on. I was in a white coat. He couldn't even see me.

The tube carrying the bug and sunflower sludge disappeared through a wall. There was a door in that wall that said, 'Authorized Personnel Only'. I had a white coat, so I figured that made me authorized personnel. I opened the door and stepped through. It was a small office. There was a guy at a desk writing at a computer. Another door in the far wall beckoned me, so I ignored the guy and crossed the room. He ignored me back.

The next room was a vast hall with a high ceiling, a steel staircase and a galleried landing at the top with a row of offices. There was a deafening noise of machines, rattling like old steam engines, coming from a complex assembly line which ran the length of two walls. I traced the pipe out of the wall and saw it fed into the end of that assembly line. They were making something out of the bug and sunflower pulp. I was curious to know what.

There were more people here, too, dressed in blue overalls with white helmets.

The blast of a horn made me look. Somebody heaved up a steel roller blind, letting in the glare of the afternoon sun and a small, reversing container truck. It stopped by a large stack of cardboard boxes and two guys started loading the boxes into the container. I strolled over, checking my clipboard, like I had something comprehensible there to look at. I glanced back the boxes. They were about two and a half feet square and had blue writing on the side. It read HEALTHFIX™.

I turned toward the end of the assembly line, where more boxes were being loaded onto pallets. I crossed the floor and as I approached I saw that what were being churned out there were small, white plastic bottles, about three inches high and two inches across. They were also labeled HEALTHFIX™. They were being packed into small, blue boxes of twelve, and these in turn were going into the big, cardboard boxes.

A health supplement. A dietary health supplement.

I picked up one of the bottles to inspect it and a voice bellowed behind me, "*Hey! Who the fuck are you?*"

Twelve

I GREW UP IN A VERY privileged family near Boston and attended the best private schools. So I usually speak with a generic east coast accent. But my mother was an English aristocrat and I spent ten years in an elite British regiment, so it is just as easy for me to switch to what the Brits call cut glass English. For some reason that was what I did right then, and it worked.

I looked at him like a dog had just left him on the sidewalk and I had accidentally stepped in him, and said, "Would you care to explain *this* to me?"

I pointed to the blue box that was now a bottle short, as I slipped the bottle into my lab coat. He didn't expect my reaction and he didn't expect my accent. He hesitated. I snapped, "I am waiting!" Before he could answer I said, "What is your name?"

Stupidity always responds to authority. His reaction was automatic. "Ferguson, sir, but..."

"Have you *any* idea of how lax security is on this plant?" I pointed at him. "I can tell you that London will *not* be impressed!"

He blanched. He hadn't known that London needed to be impressed. But now that he did, he was worried. He was out of his depth and beginning to panic. I sighed. I was clearly losing patience. "I can't waste time on your incompetence! Where is your supervisor?"

"In the... he's... but you..."

"Take me to him *immediately!*"

He looked relived and nodded. "Yes, this way."

He walked quickly, like a man who is trying to get away from a responsibility, and doesn't know he is hurrying into the arms of his executioner. We were approaching a prefab office against one wall. Through the window I could see a man at a desk. He was looking down, either at a screen or at some papers. There was nobody else with him. The whole place seemed to be run with a minimum of personnel. What military personnel there was was all around the perimeter, keeping people out. But on the inside there was practically nobody. Both facts made sense.

My guide looked at me nervously as we approached the door.

"I will need to tell Mr. Price your name..."

I snapped, "Epsilon!" and he shut up.

Ferguson knocked on the door. A lazy voice said, "Come in," without looking up and we stepped through into the office. Ferguson opened his mouth to speak and I shot him through the vertebra at the base of his skull. He never even knew that he'd been killed. He is probably still wandering around the plant, wondering why nobody will talk to him.

Mr. Price frowned and looked up when he heard Ferguson hit the floor. By that time I was sitting on the corner of his desk with the Sig on my lap pointed at his crotch. A direct threat to a man's crotch will tend to make him cooperative. He turned very pale and asked me, "Who are you? What do you want?"

I can be a wiseass sometimes, so I did my best imitation of Colin Firth and said, "Now is not the time for existential questions, Mr. Price. Now is the time for you to give me your shipping ledger."

"What?"

I smiled and glanced over at Ferguson. I looked back into Price's eyes and let the smile slip. "Don't try to understand, Mr. Price. Just do as I tell you and you might leave this place without exploring the existential mysteries in depth. Am I being too abstruse for you, Mr. Price? Would you like me to be more direct?"

"No!" He pointed at a shelf behind me. "I have to get it..."

I nodded and he stood carefully and walked to the shelf. "What period?"

I shrugged. "The most recent. Put it on the desk."

He returned with a large, black lever arch file and placed it in front of me. I said, "Sit. Explain."

He was sweating and his hands were shaking. He opened the file and started to talk.

"This covers the period from last January to the present. Here it lists all the shipments out of the plant, here are their destinations, quantities, and at the back, here, are the manifests for each shipment."

"How much does Maddox pay you to keep quiet about this stuff?"

He swallowed hard, but his eyes had turned shifty. "Mr. Maddox is a very generous employer. Are you a cop?"

I raised an eyebrow. "What if I am?"

"You talk funny."

"I'm CIA."

He spoke in a rush, like verbal diarrhea, "I'll turn state's evidence. I'll tell you everything you need to know. Cut me a deal and I'll give you the whole lot."

I shot him between the eyes. Now he could explain to Ferguson what had happened. I picked up the ledger and walked out. I needed to find out what these damned tablets were, and I had a hunch I would get that information in the huts. But I also had a hunch I was running out of time. Three bodies so far, and sooner or later somebody was going to find one of them.

I crossed the hall again and went back through the small office. The guy at the computer was still there. He stretched and yawned and said something to me and laughed. I smiled grimly and said, "You got that right." And carried on through.

I was back in the unloading area where the conveyor belt was. My truck was gone and a new one had taken its place. I could see the driver still in the cab, reading a magazine. I walked purposefully toward the entrance holding the ledger under my arm like I was engaged in some important job. As I passed through the doors, I glanced under the conveyor belt, saw that my bag was still there and wondered if I would soon need it. Something told me I would.

The first of the green huts was about fifty yards from the hangar. I could see the wire fence, and beyond it, the armed guards patrolling it with dogs—Rottweilers and Alsatians. I glanced around. There were four or five people, mostly in blue coveralls, and they were all doing their own thing. They didn't seem to be aware of me. I walked, gazing down like I was working out some knotty problem involved in making pills out of sunflowers, and came eventually to the first of the huts. The door was open, so I stepped inside.

I was in a lab. It was like a cross between a lab and a green-house. There were a lot of electronic machines that to my un-educated eye looked like mass spectrometers, powerful micro-scopes and DNA sequencers. There were others which I could not identify. There was a long table down the center of the room that held racks of test tubes and the kind of toys Profes-sor Frankenstein might have got excited about. Lying on this table were a number of sunflowers and glass jars of varying sizes. I drew closer to have a look. I wasn't surprised to see that the jars mostly contained the small, golden bugs. Some were dead, others were alive.

I strolled along a few steps and a man entered from the far end, where the lab joined at right angles with another hut. He was tall and stooping, with heavy glasses. And he was wearing a lab coat, like mine. He looked a little surprised to see me. I smiled at him and continued looking at the things on the bench. He said, "Weitz, I don't think I know you."

"Zwally, I'm visiting. How's it going?"

He shrugged and spread his hands. "We're going to have to wait for the field results before we can make any kind of deter-mination. For now it *looks* hopeful and the first trials *seem* to indicate a drop in activity in the prefrontal cortex. But as I say, until we get the results from the field tests it is impossible to be more definite." He paused. "Don't mind me asking, but are you a scientist or are you from administration? Normally I am in-formed..."

I took a few steps closer and sighed like that wasn't an easy question to answer. "My background is in science, Weitz, and I confess that is where my interest lies. But I was roped into ad-ministration. So they have me paying visits to make sure things are staying on track, on budget and on time." He grunted and I sighed again. "But personally I don't think science works like that. Am I right?"

"You're not wrong." He had sat at a microscope and was adjusting the lens as he peered into it. He had clearly lost interest in me. My mind was racing. A drop in the activity of the prefrontal cortex was ringing bells in my memory. I said, "Essentially we are talking about an action not dissimilar to sodium thiopental."

He laughed without humor, as though I had been absurdly simplistic.

"At its very simplest, you could say so, but the potential here goes far, far beyond sodium thiopental. This is like the ion drive to the combustion engine."

I leaned against the table and shrugged. "Sure, but I mean, in principle, it is basically the same thing, right?"

He looked up from the microscope and turned to face me, like I was getting on his nerves.

"In that it interferes with the neural activity in the prefrontal cortex, yes. But it goes so far beyond that. We are talking about inhibiting neural networks that are engaged in subjective, moral thought. Have you any idea what that means?" He laughed in a way that said I was stupid. "We are stimulating networks that recognize and obey authority. Have you any conception of what *that* means - for *society?*" He shook his head. "No, my dear Zwally. This goes very far beyond sodium thiopental."

He turned back to his microscope. I nodded. "Sure, of course, I see that." I opened the ledger and said, "Remind me now, you head up..."

He stopped what he was doing and stared down at his bench. I knew I had overplayed my hand and started working out what my strategy was going to be. He turned to face me and narrowed his eyes. "I lead the research here, Zwally, and you would know that if you were visiting from Admin."

"Of course I would, if I were visiting from Admin..."

"So who the hell are you?"

The voice came from behind me and I knew I was seriously fucked.

"His name is Lacklan Walker, Dr Weitz, and he is a very dangerous man. Make one move, Walker, and you will be shot dead where you stand. Now put your hands in the air and turn to face me."

I put the ledger on the lower shelf of the bench, raised my hands and turned to face Maddox. He wasn't taking any chances. He was holding a semi-automatic and he had six armed guards with him, all pointing assault rifles at me. He snapped, "Cuff him! Take him to the truck depot."

They all six advanced on me. One of them yanked my arms behind my back and slapped a pair of cuffs on me. When he was done, the one in front of me smacked me in the jaw with the butt of his rifle and put my lights out.

Thirteen

I WOKE UP WITH THE feeling that somebody had stuck a steel girder in my skull and was jumping up and down on it for fun. There were various other pains too, like dull blades being threaded through my chest. I opened my eyes and slowly the stabbing pains in my chest began to make sense. I was hanging by my wrists and my lungs were beginning to go into spasm. I groped with my feet to find something to stand on, but there was nothing.

I raised my eyes. My wrists had been duct-taped together and slipped over an iron hook that was suspended by a chain from a steel girder. I looked around. I was in a large garage-cum-depot. There was a truck over to one side with the hood up. Just beyond it there was a small office. On my left, there was a stack of fuel drums by the entrance. And standing in the entrance were three silhouettes smoking. One of them was Maddox. Another I didn't know—a guy in a suit with black shades. The third was his driver. That wasn't good news.

Duct tape is a really useful tool for quickly and effectively immobilizing somebody. But it has one drawback. If you can nick it in just the right place, it will rip very easily. Trouble was, the way I was hanging, it was going to be almost impossible for me to do that, because it was holding all my weight, and I could barely move my hands.

I saw Maddox turn and look at me. He said something to the other two and they threw down their cigarettes and crossed the floor toward me. Their steps and their voices had a strange, metallic echo in the dark, cavernous building. Maddox spoke first.

"I'm going to make this simple, Walker. I made you an offer and you turned me down. Now I am going to kill you. The choice you have is to die quickly and painlessly, or die slowly and in pain. Tell me what I want to know and I will put a bullet in the back of your head, give me trouble and I will have you sobbing and begging for your mommy."

I smiled. He didn't know my mother. "How about if I tell you more than you want to know?"

He frowned. "What are you talking about?"

"You're seeing the small picture, Maddox. You're thinking about Marni and her father, you're not thinking about the people who might have got behind them in the last twenty years; the people who might have got behind Marni while she was at Harvard."

He glanced at the guy in the suit and confirmed my suspicion. I directed my words to him now.

"Think about it. You think an operative of my class is cheap? My father was fond of Marni, but you think a son of a bitch like him would put himself at risk to help her? You think you were the only people who noticed her research? You think nobody *else* noticed she was following in her father's footsteps?"

Maddox was squinting at my face. "What are you saying?"

"Uh-uh. I want a third option. I can be damn useful to you, Maddox. You haven't got a single man who is up to my standard."

The guy in the shades smirked. "Said the guy hanging from the meat hook."

"I ain't dead yet, pal, which is more than can be said for seven of your men. And I haven't got started yet."

"Cut the crap. Where is the girl?"

"Give me a third option and I'll tell you."

Maddox shook his head. "You are in no position to negotiate." He turned to his driver. "Don't kill him. We'll drag this out till Christmas if we have to." He turned back to me. "We'll start with beatings. After that we'll start removing things." To his driver he said, "Call me the instant he offers to speak, understand?"

"Sure thing, Mr. Maddox."

The guy was as strong as he was stupid, and he was really very stupid. He started by pounding my ribs and my stomach, which made me vomit. That is surprisingly hard to do when you are suspended by your wrists. It is also hard to tense against the blows when you are strung up like that. All I could do was take it, and ride the pain. After ten or twelve blows, when I was lingering between nausea and unconsciousness, he went behind me and delivered two shattering punches just below my shoulder blades. The pain was indescribable. My lungs went into spasm and because of the position I was in I could not breathe. I felt myself on the edge of panic and my breath rasped in my throat as I kicked with my feet and tried to haul myself up to relieve my lungs.

The son of a bitch laughed. He must have realized I was approaching cardiac arrest because he took hold of my legs in a kind of bear hug and raised me enough to let air into my lungs. Then he dropped me, sending shards of pain piercing through my lungs again. As I gasped he slapped my face with his open hand, enough to hurt but not enough to stun or numb me. I began to wonder how long I could hold out.

He gave me a few more back-handers, then turned and walked away. After five minutes he came back with a piece of wood about five feet long, two inches thick. Then he settled down to beating me with it on my arms and on my legs. I have no idea how long it went on. It may have been half an hour, it may have been an hour. In the end I had the strange experience of being completely numb in a world of pain. I could hear myself groaning, but I didn't realize it was me.

Somewhere in the fog of agony I heard Maddox's voice telling his driver to stop. "Is he alive? I told you not to kill him!"

"I owed him, Mr. Maddox..."

"You damn fool! Get him down! If he's dead..."

I felt myself being lifted down and laid on the floor. Maddox knelt and slapped my face. "Bring some water."

I was in pain. But the gorilla's beating had been more skillful than Maddox realized. I was nowhere near death. The ape had done exactly what his boss had told him to do, but he was too stupid to know how to tell him. I acted up, moaning like I was delirious and slipping into coma. It would at least give me a chance to recover.

I felt myself drifting, heard a shambling of feet as though from another room, or another world, and then the shock of cold water made me gasp and choke. I was wide awake now, but weak and still in a lot of pain. I rolled my eyes and moaned like I was half dead. Maddox said, "Give him a couple of hours, then we'll start cutting bits off." Then his voice grew louder. "You'd better have recovered by then, Walker. Being able to talk is the only thing standing between you and weeks of excruciating pain. Think about that." To the Ape Man he said, "Keep an eye on him. I'll send someone to relieve you in an hour. And for fuck's sake, don't do any more to him."

I gave them fifteen seconds, then opened my eyes. Maddox was gone and so was the guy in the suit. The Ape Man was over by the door, sitting on a drum of diesel, smoking a cigarette. I gave myself another thirty seconds to recover my strength and looked around me for something sharp. About five feet from my head there was a dirty steel trolley. I could see several tools poking out from the top shelf, but I didn't want to risk standing up in the state I was in. On the lower shelf I could see a screwdriver. I quietly reached out with my arms, but I couldn't quite make it. I braced my feet and pushed. I slid a foot. I looked at Ape Man. He was examining the tip of his cigarette, like he was trying to remember how it got there.

I braced my feet again and gave another push. My fingers touched the blue plastic handle. I eased it gently into my hands, then slowly pulled myself back to where they had left me on the floor.

I turned the tool over so the blade was facing in, resting on the duct tape, nudged the tip under the edge of the tape, and pressed hard. It bit, resisted and then split. I groaned loudly and made an incoherent noise. Ape Man turned to look at me. I groaned again.

He dropped his cigarette and trod on it, then shambled back toward me.

"You ready to talk?"

I gazed at him with unfocused eyes and made pasty noises with my mouth, like I was trying to say something. He bent down to hear me. I leaned toward him. He came closer. I had the screwdriver up my right sleeve. I grabbed his lapel with my left, yanked hard and rammed the screwdriver through his windpipe. It wasn't enough to kill him, but as he began to choke on his own blood, it was enough to incapacitate him while I staggered to my feet and found a tire iron. I put a lot of rage into the first blow. It knocked him on his face, but he was tough and he was still alive. I had to stamp twice with the blade of my foot on the back of his neck before he finally let go and died.

If a job is worth doing, I figure it's worth doing well, so I stamped again twice, just for the sake of completeness.

Outside, dusk was closing in. I took a couple of seconds to breathe deep, then made my way to the small office on the other side of the truck. My knife, my Sig and my phone were on the desk, which was a bit odd. Just how stupid were these guys? Maybe they weren't stupid. Maybe they were over-confident.

I took a moment to think about what to do next. I needed to retrieve the ledger, a sample of the pills and a sample of the bugs, and get them all to Marni so she would know exactly what had been going on here, and how far they were distributing it. But that wouldn't satisfy me. Not by a long chalk. Before I left, I wanted them to know they had a problem. I also wanted to keep them busy while I found Marni and got her somewhere safe. And I knew exactly how to do that. I went to look for a blow torch.

Fourteen

I HAD THREE-QUARTERS of an hour to wait before Ape Man's replacement arrived. That gave me time to recover my strength and work out the details of what I had to do. I was waiting, sitting behind the door when he arrived. He was whistling a jaunty tune. He'd obviously been having a good day up to that point.

I shot him in the left hip. He gasped, like somebody who has stepped into a really cold shower. Then he folded over to the left and kept saying, "Oh God! Oh shit! Shit...!"

I went and grabbed him by the scruff of the neck and dragged him over where we wouldn't be seen by passers-by. I frisked him and found a Glock 19. It was a girl's gun, but I stuck it in my waistband and picked up the blowtorch. He saw it and began to panic, holding out his hands and saying, "No, no, no..."

I looked him in the eye. "I am going to burn your face off."

"No, no please, anything, what do you want? I'll cooperate." He had tears in his eyes from the fear and the pain. I almost felt sorry for him.

"Where is Maddox?"

"In the main office. In the factory. Mister, I need a doctor."

"Where they make the pills?"

He nodded.

I said, "What about the guy in the suit and the shades?"

He knew who I meant. "He's with him." He was whimpering.

"Who is he?"

"I don't know his name. They don't use names. They just call him Tau."

"Tau?" He nodded. It made sense. Tau was the nineteenth letter of the Greek alphabet. "What else?"

He shrugged. He was crying now, his face creased up. "He's from the Omega Corporation. They say he's Maddox's boss, please Mister, it really hurts."

"OK, what about Dr. Weitz? Where is he?"

"He's always in the labs, just out here on the left. You can't miss it. Please let me get a doctor. I ain't nobody. I am just..."

I cut across him. "You're just the guy who was going to torture me for the next four months." I shot him in the head. Like I said, I hadn't completely lost my humanity.

I took the blow torch and lit it. Then I carried it over and placed it a couple of inches from the barrel at the middle of the stack of diesel drums. Diesel is not flammable, it's combustible. That means it won't burn, but when it gets hot it releases gases that are explosive. I didn't know how long it would take, but eventually that drum would blow.

I was mad as hell by now, and in no mood for creeping around. I walked up to the nearest hut and kicked the door in. There were three lab technicians. They looked at me in surprise. I shot two of them between the eyes and kicked the third in the nuts. As he went down wheezing, I put the Sig to his head and said, "Where is Weitz?"

He looked up at me and pointed toward the next hut. I shot him and moved on.

I found Weitz with one of his colleagues poring over some graphics on a computer. I shot the colleague and his brains made a mess of the screen. Weitz gave a scream like a woman and tried to stand. I came up close, grabbed his hair and smashed his face against the bloody screen. Then I dragged him backward onto the table and stuck the silenced muzzle of the Sig in his mouth.

"I am going to blow a hole through the back of your neck and sever your spinal cord. Then I am going to set fire to this place and leave you to burn, you mother fucker, unless you tell me right now what this fucking operation is about."

He gurgled and I removed the weapon from his mouth. He started burbling. "You can't! You don't understand! It's..."

I blew his kneecap off. He screamed hysterically, clawing at my shirt. I put the muzzle on his other knee and spoke quietly. "If you prefer I can ask somebody else."

"You don't understand. You can't do this. It goes beyond..."

I blew his other kneecap off and threw him on the floor. I picked up a jar of bugs and pushed my way out. I'd be back to deal with him after I got my kit bag. I found the ledger in the next hut and made my way toward the big hangar doors.

There was a truck unloading and I slipped behind it. My bag was where I had left it, under the conveyor belt. I dropped the ledger and the bugs into it and pulled out a cake of C4 and tore it in half. I shaped one and stuck it to the bottom of the conveyor with a remote detonator in it. The other I stuck under the cab of the truck with a universal firing mechanism, which I attached to the edge of the conveyor frame. When he tried to reverse out, it would be the last thing he ever did. I slung the bag over my shoulder and started across the hangar floor toward the factory. It wasn't the foreman's lucky day. He saw me and shouted.

"*Hey! Who the fuck are you? Where the fuck...?*"

He didn't get any further. I shot him between the eyes and kept walking. I kicked in the office door. This time the guy at the computer looked up. He shouldn't have. I shot him through the eye.

In the big hall with the assembly line, I stopped and looked around. The only people I could see were at a table packing the bottles of pills into boxes. I dumped my bag on the floor and shaped six charges with remote detonators. It was enough to blow the whole damn hangar to hell. Then I pulled the Smith & Wesson 500 from the bag with a spare box of 500 grain slugs. These things will smash a cinderblock to dust. I was feeling pretty mad.

I climbed the stairs. Maddox's office was the first. I blew out the lock and in the process ripped the door off its hinges and shattered the two plate glass windows. Maddox and Tau were sitting around a coffee table drinking whiskey. They stared at me the way people do when their brain is telling them something is seriously wrong with reality.

The 500 has a kick like a mule on steroids. You need to hold it with both hands. I took a whole second to aim. They both goggled in horrified fascination. I pulled the trigger and Maddox's head exploded like a watermelon all over the wall behind him.

Tau said, "Oh, Jesus!" and made to stand.

I said, "Don't." He froze. I went on, "I didn't need him because I have you. Don't make me regret my decision."

"OK, take it easy, we can talk about this..."

"Don't patronize me or you'll make me mad. I lose my sense of proportion when I'm mad."

"What do you want?"

"We are going to the limo. You're going to drive."

He nodded and stood up. I grabbed him by the scruff of the neck and dragged him out of the office. When we got to the top of the stairs, I threw him down, following him at a run and kicking him every time he tried to stand. At the bottom, I dragged him to his feet. "Which way?" He pointed toward a steel roller blind that stood open. I shoved him. "You've seen what this baby can do, Tau. Don't try and run or I swear I'll cut you in half."

The limo was parked just outside. He pulled the keys from his pocket and opened it. I gestured at him with the gun and said, "Turn around."

He did as I said and I knocked him out cold. I took the keys and his shoelaces and tied his ankles together and his wrists behind his back. Then I shoved him in the trunk. I had a couple more things to do before I was ready to leave. I took four more cakes of C4 and eight remote detonators, and returned to the huts. I distributed them evenly, but pretty much at random. Weitz was unconscious. I made a point of leaving one a couple of feet away from where he was lying.

As I was returning to the limo, I heard the reverse gears of a truck grinding in the hangar. A couple of seconds later, the whole place was rocked by the explosion and black smoke started to billow out of the hangar doors. I climbed in the car and started driving west toward the fields. After thirty seconds or a minute, streams of guards on foot and in Jeeps started passing me on the way toward the hangar. All their focus had been on the outside, to keep people like me out. While the security on the inside, where I was, had been negligible. The two guards at the gate saw the limo speeding toward them, recognized the car and opened up to let us through.

I skidded to a halt on the outside as the gates closed behind me. I pulled the Heckler and Koch from my bag and stepped out into the glare of the spotlights. The two guards frowned, uncomprehending. I put three rounds into each of them.

After that, I took one more cake of C4, molded it and stuck it under the gas tank, then I drove the limo into the nearest sunflower plantation, climbed out and dragged Tau from the trunk. I threw him on the ground and pointed the Smith & Wesson at his right knee. He was sweating and shaking badly.

"I have very little time, Tau. You get one chance. Don't blow it. What are you doing here?"

He didn't answer for a moment. He hesitated. I cocked the revolver and he shied away. "No! Wait! It's complicated. This is just part of it. The beetles, they contain a natural acid, like LSD, only in small doses it isn't hallucinogenic. It triggers dopamine production in the brain, but it also inhibits the activity in the frontal cortex."

"Plain English, I'm running out of time."

"OK, it makes people obedient and stops them from thinking, plus, they enjoy it."

"Are there other plants like this?"

He shook his head. "No, this was experimental."

"The pills you're shipping out...?"

"We are testing them on the population as a whole, to see how people react. It's tied in with social media and..."

He heard it at the same time I did. Jeeps speeding back. The gates were closed and that would delay them. Tau was still tied up. I grabbed my kit bag and sprinted for the nearest fence.

It took me thirty seconds of hard running to get there. I blew a hole in the wires with the Smith & Wesson and scrambled through. I looked back and saw two Jeeps pulling up near Tau. I couldn't see him. I pulled my cell from my pocket, pressed speed dial 9, counted one and a half seconds, and watched all hell break loose. The hangar shuddered and belched fire. The diesel that had been heating was ignited by the shock wave and erupted like a volcano, spewing fire, black smoke and spiraling drums across the enclosure. The laboratory huts erupted in flames, sending shattered wood spiraling into the air.

Closer, the fuel tank in the limo exploded, sending the car somersaulting and spraying burning fuel over the forests of giant flowers. They caught and the flames started to roar. A wave of heat washed over me, making me shield my face with my arms. I didn't know if the fire would destroy them all. I could only hope.

I headed back, leaving the wild conflagration behind me, the flames reaching high up into the night sky. I looked south and east, up into the hills, knowing that Marni was looking down at the fire, knowing I had done what she had wanted me to do.

Fifteen

I DESPERATELY NEEDED to rest, but I couldn't. Not yet. Instead of retracing my steps south and east toward Turret and the diner, I followed the road in a roughly easterly direction, making for Marni's cabin. I knew the fire would be spotted, and before long choppers and planes would be flying over, attempting to stop it spreading. But I figured the road would be safe for at least another couple of hours, probably more.

I was walking in a kind of trance. As the adrenaline boost wore off, every inch of my body was beginning to ache from the beating I had received. I didn't know how much longer I could keep going, so I just focused on the next step, and then the next, and somehow I made it to the track that led up through the woods to her cabin.

Climbing was harder, and I had to stop several times to rest. The thought that she would be there, waiting, kept me going. I hadn't allowed myself to dwell on it since I had left my father's house, but now I wondered, as I climbed, why she had left that photograph pinned to the board. A photograph she knew only I could recognize. What was the message she was trying to send me? On the surface it was a cry for help. But on a deeper level, it meant more. It must mean more. It meant that she knew I would come. That she trusted me and believed in me.

The trees closed in and the darkness grew more dense. Sounds became magnified: the rustle of small animals in the undergrowth, the flutter of wings of an owl, the distant cry of a coyote, my own footsteps, too loud over the dead leaves, tramping on the path.

The track finally leveled off. My legs were shaking and my breathing was ragged. Over to the right I saw the cabin. There was no light in the window, but I didn't expect there would be. I moved toward it and a shape stepped out in front of me, about ten or twelve feet away. Automatically my hand slipped behind my back for the Sig. Then I heard her voice.

"Lacklan...?"

"Yeah, it's me."

I moved toward her and we clung to each other. But after a second, she was grabbing my hand and pulling me. "Come inside, quick!"

I pulled her back. "Marni, it's over. They are all dead."

She shook her head. "No, they are not."

"What are you talking about?"

"There are hundreds of them. Please come, quickly! We haven't much time."

I followed her up the porch steps and we slipped inside. She had a fire burning and one lamp turned low. But she had heavy drapes over the window, so the light was not visible from the outside.

She closed the door and slipped the bolt, then turned to face me. I smiled. It had been a long time, and I hadn't realized how much I had missed her. She looked drawn and put a hand to her mouth.

"What have they done to you?"

"It doesn't matter. I told you. They are all dead."

"They hurt you. I am so sorry..."

"Don't be." I looked her in the eye. "I'm glad you left the message, the photograph."

She smiled and took a small step closer. "I knew you'd recognize it."

The exhaustion was getting to me and I was beginning to feel weak. She saw it and reached for me. "Come and sit. I have some fresh coffee brewing."

I sat on the sofa, and while she went to get coffee, I pulled the ledger, the bugs and the pills from the bag.

"I brought these. I thought you could use them."

She approached, frowning, carrying the coffee pot and two mugs. I poured while she looked at them.

"What are they?"

"I'm not sure. I couldn't get a lot out of them. Apart from Maddox and Tau, there was some kind of nutty professor, a guy called Weitz. What I put together from what they told me was that it's marketed as a health supplement, but what it does is to reduce the function of the frontal cortex..."

"The part of the mind involved in intellectual processes, critical thinking..."

"Exactly. It also stimulates dopamine and the processes in the brain that make people obey authority." I pointed at the jar of bugs. "Apparently whatever this chemical is, they derive it from that bug." I picked up the ledger. "And this lists all the places where they have been distributing it as part of a field test."

She took the ledger from me and leafed through it. After a bit she sighed and put it down again.

"Lacklan, this is so much bigger, more complex, than you can imagine."

"What are you telling me?"

She shook her head. "I haven't time to tell you anything. You have to go."

I frowned. "Now?"

"Yes."

"I don't get it. Did you not see the fire? I burned the crops. I destroyed the factory where they were making the pills. I destroyed the lab where they were carrying out their research. I killed Maddox, Tau and Weitz." I shrugged. "It's over."

She sat forward and took hold of my hand. "Lacklan, Maddox was not part of the organization..."

"Omega."

"You know about Omega?"

"My father told me."

She was pensive for a moment, then sighed again and went on, "Maddox was not Omega, he was being used by Omega. The only Omega representatives there were Professor Weitz and Tau. If you have killed them you have done the world a great service. Those men are pure evil. But they are hard to kill, and the Omega organization is much, much bigger than that farm, or those two men, believe me."

I felt a sudden rush of anger. "Then what the hell have I done all this for?"

"No, listen to me. What you have done is fantastic. You have hurt them and you have delayed their research. That is incredibly important. But it is not the end. It is only the beginning. And they will be coming for us both."

"Fuck them!" I stood up. "Let them come! We'll go back to Boston, or new York. We'll go to the media and expose them. We'll give the evidence to the FBI..."

She stood and held my face in her hands. "Lacklan, *please* listen to me. These people control the media, they can influence the courts and they have powerful people in the FBI. They are an infection that feeds on power, and they have tendrils everywhere. There is a way to do this, but you have to trust me and believe that I know what I am talking about."

I took hold of her shoulders and stared into her eyes. "I don't want to let you go again. If you are in danger, I have to protect you."

"Lacklan, we haven't time. Trust me. I know what I am doing. You have to go, or we will both be killed."

"So...when will I see you again? What happens now?"

"Soon. What happens now is that you go, quickly! If they catch us together, we are finished."

I took my kit bag and she followed me to the door. She reached up and kissed me.

"Now, *go!*"

I stepped out into the night and made my way back down the track. I was sure she was wrong. I *knew* she was wrong. I was too tired to think it through, but there was no way they could recover from the damage I had done to them that night. No way.

As I came out from the tree cover into the light of the rising full moon, I saw the blaze of light over in the northwest and smiled to myself. Far off I could hear the throb of a chopper and the buzz of planes dumping tons of water onto the burning complex.

Halfway down the track I heard a different noise. It was the wail of sirens. I slipped off the road and lay down among the shrubs behind a tree. Thirty seconds later a whole convoy sped past, with sirens blaring, headed toward what was left of the farm. The sheriff's Ford pick-up was in the lead, followed by two deputies. Then there were two fire trucks and three cars from the state police.

There would be more. And it was time I disappeared. That was clear.

I scrambled down the rest of the slope and ran across the road. Then I made my way back to the diner cross-country, keeping to the wooded areas and below the crest of the highlands. I finally got back to Turret at two AM. I let myself in through the back door and went through to the bar. I realized I was starving, but I was too tired to make any food. I grabbed a bottle of Irish and a glass and collapsed into a chair. I poured myself a generous measure and drained the glass. Then I poured another and pulled a packet of Camels from my pocket. I lit up, took a long, deep drag, and sighed.

I heard a noise and looked up. Blueberry was standing in the door that led to the stairs. Her eyes were puffy, either from sleep or lack of it. She gave something that wanted to be a smile.

"You're alive."

"I think so. Just about."

"Did you eat?"

"The restaurant was closed."

"What did you do, Lacklan?"

I looked at her for a long moment, then shrugged. "It's better you don't know, baby."

"You hungry?"

I nodded and she went to the kitchen. Soon I heard the sound of frying, and I smelled bacon and singed steak. I drifted for a couple of minutes and she woke me with a plate of bacon, steak and fries. I poured her a glass of whiskey and ate hungrily while she watched and smoked and drank.

When I'd finished, I took her up to my room.

Sixteen

I WOKE UP TO SEE THE sun streaming through my window. For a moment I had a sense of panic. I sat up and reached for my watch. It was ten AM. I had overslept and I needed to be on the move. I stood and seven different types of pain wracked my body from my head down to the soles of my feet.

I went to the bathroom and stood under a stream of cold water for ten minutes, then soaped myself and washed my hair. When I stepped out again, I felt better. Not good, but better.

As I toweled myself dry, I heard voices downstairs. It was the sheriff. I dressed quickly, put a fresh magazine in the Sig and slipped it in my waistband behind my back. Then I crept halfway down the stairs to listen.

Blueberry was talking. Her voice was loud and strident.

"I'm telling you, Sheriff, there was something wrong with that man. He gave me the creeps. Last time I saw him, let me think, was yesterday, when you come 'round and he hit poor Mr. Maddox's driver. After you'd gone he upped and left. Never so much as paid his goddamn bill. I don't *know* what I'm going to tell Mom and Daddy!"

The sheriff's deeper drawl cut in. "Well if he comes back, Blueberry, you just make sure and call me. You understand?"

"Don't you worry about that, Sheriff. If he so much as shows his face 'round here I'll be on the phone to you."

I heard the door bang and sprinted back up the stairs to peer out of the window. I saw the sheriff's pick-up and two deputies' cars waiting outside. The sheriff was leaning on one of them talking through the window. Two ambulances crawled by with their lights flashing, then accelerated away toward Salida. I saw the sheriff stand erect and hitch up his pants, like he was watching somebody approaching. I angled myself and saw a black limo turn into the street from North Spring Road. It was not a Caddie, but an Audi. It pulled up in front of the sheriff.

I was frowning. Was it the Feds? Was it somebody from Omega who had driven in this morning while I was sleeping? There might have been another limo at the plant, but who the hell was left to drive it?

The driver got out. He was in a suit, but he had that unmistakable military bearing. He had a crew cut and aviator shades. He also had a lot of bruises and cuts. He walked around the car and opened the back door. The man who got out had his arm in a sling. Part of his face was bandaged and his skin was a livid red color in patches. But the son of a bitch was alive. Tau had survived the bomb and the resulting firestorm.

I reached for my kit bag on the floor and pulled out my assault rifle. I went to the window and was about to haul it open and finish the job, but Blueberry's voice came from behind me.

"Don't do it, Lacklan."

I turned to face her.

"They've been driving through all morning, going to the farm and coming back. I don't know what the hell you did last night, but there must be over a hundred cops there. If you kill him now, they'll kill both of us."

I looked back out the window. Tau was staring up at the diner. He seemed to sigh, said something to the sheriff and climbed back in his car. It took off and the sheriff and deputies followed after him.

A feeling of dread washed over me. I turned to Blueberry. "Let me borrow your car for an hour."

She sighed, reached in her pocket and threw me the keys. I glanced out the window. The street was clear. I ran down the stairs and out onto the porch. The road was still empty. I leapt over the rail and climbed into her small Toyota. Then I hit the gas and took off toward Marni's cabin. I knew what I was going to find, but I had to see it for myself. I didn't bother to hide the dust trail. The time for hiding was long past. What I needed now was speed.

I turned onto the track and probably wrecked her suspension doing fifty MPH over rocks and potholes until I skidded to a halt outside the cabin. I scrambled out and ran. As I did so, I noted the ground had been churned up by at least four sets of tires. I ripped open the door and went in.

The coffee pot was on the floor. The pool of coffee around it had not yet dried. The mugs she and I had drunk from that night were overturned and the coffee table had been yanked aside. There was nothing else, but the story it told was clear. They had burst in. She had tried to run and they had snatched her. She had probably been in the Audi with Tau.

Next time I saw him, I promised myself, next time I saw him I would not stop until I had torn his heart from his chest.

I left the cabin and headed up the hill at a run. My legs were screaming and my lungs were screaming louder, but I wasn't listening. I needed to get to the Hole in the Wall. I needed to see if she had left anything for me there, any clue, any message, anything that might help.

I reached the small plateau and had to stop. My bruised ribs, from where the Ape Man had beaten me the day before, felt like they were going to split. I continued, scrambling over rocks and stumbling on the loose stones until I was able to jump down into the hollow.

I peered in the cave. There was nothing new. Nothing had been disturbed. It was as I had last seen it. I caught my breath and started the slipping, sliding descent toward the tree. With my heart pounding, partly from the exertion and partly out of fear of what they would do to Marni if I didn't get to her in time, I crawled under the lower branches of the old pine and began to dig. I pulled up the board and looked inside the hole.

The ledger was not there, because it would not fit. But the contents of the ledger, rolled up and sealed in a plastic bag, were there. So were the pills and the jar of bugs. The Sig 232 was gone.

I covered it again and sat, with my back against the ancient trunk and tried to think. How? How had they found her? The very reason they'd given me the beating was to try and find out where she was. I had razed the place to the ground and escaped. And within a few hours they had found her.

Then it came back to me. I had been exhausted, too tired and too much in pain to think clearly. But even so, it had struck me as strange at the time. My gun, my knife and my phone right there, waiting for me. I pulled my cell from my pocket and opened it up. There it was, right by the SIM card. Another fucking tracking device. They had only expected me to escape.

They had not expected me to destroy their entire complex. But even so, I had led them right to her.

I took my time going back, turning over in my mind the possibilities. I had no idea where they might take her, and as far as I could see, I had lost any chance of finding out. I came to the cabin and leaned on the roof of the car, looking out across the treetops at the long trail of smoke that lingered on the afternoon air.

No way of finding out where she was, unless...

I climbed in the car and drove back to the diner at a more leisurely pace.

I pushed in to the dark, quiet room. Blueberry was leaning on the bar looking bored.

"You killed all my clients, you fucking asshole."

I grabbed the phone and said, "All except one. Make me a burger, will you?"

I dialed the number I had memorized. It rang twice and a rather prissy voice said, "Don't say anything. I'll call you back."

I hung up and fifteen seconds later the phone rang. I picked it up and the same voice said, "I know who you are. Don't use any names. This is a secure line. The call has been rerouted through one hundred and fifty countries, but still, it's best to be safe. How can I help you?"

"Somebody put a tracking device in my phone, so they could follow me. Can we reverse that and find out where the receiver is?"

He was silent for a moment, then he said, "Yes, we can do that. Can you pick me up from Colorado Springs tomorrow, at the airport?"

"Yes. How did you know...?"

"Your phone number. Give me your cell number too. Just wait for me in the parking lot. I'll find you. Just bear with me..." I heard him rattling at a keyboard. After a couple of minutes he said, "OK, one-thirty PM."

I gave him my cell number and he hung up.

Blueberry was leaning on the kitchen doorjamb looking at me. She looked depressed.

"I'll make it right, Blueberry."

"That's what they all say."

"I do what I say."

She smiled ruefully. "I guess you do, at that."

Seventeen

COLORADO SPRINGS AIRPORT is on the eastern edge of town, on the Milton E Proby Parkway, and has a very large parking lot. I used the Zombie and made the trip in good time, though I took it easy. I didn't want to draw any attention to myself. I pulled in off the parkway and found a spot as close to the airport as I could. It was one-fifteen. At one-forty I saw a guy walking toward me. He was thin, dressed in the same jeans and sweatshirt he'd probably been wearing for the last six weeks, and his blond hair hung all the way down to his waist. He was carrying a metal, reinforced attaché case and looked like somebody NASA would probably employ.

He opened the door and climbed in the passenger seat. I stared at him as he opened his briefcase and held out his hand to me. The case was, as I had imagined, a computer.

"Is the tracker still fitted to your phone?"

"How can you be so sure it's me?"

"Let's not waste time."

"Yes, it's still fitted to my phone."

"May I have it, please?"

I handed him the cell and he connected it to a USB which then plugged into the PC.

"OK," he said, "It's still transmitting. If it had stopped transmitting that would have been a problem. But it is still sending a signal, so, with the right software, we can follow that signal." He rattled at the keyboard and then paused. "OK, we are connecting."

"You owe my father a favor?"

"I'm sorry." He was staring at the screen. "I don't want to talk about that."

"I'd like to pay you for your services. I don't want to accept anything from my father."

"I hear you, but I can't accept. While we wait, let's talk about something. I gather you want to go after these people?"

I nodded. "Yes."

"Then it would be helpful for you if they thought you were somewhere else."

"Of course."

"So after I have identified where the receiver is, here is what we are going to do. This transmitter is operating through your telephone, not through your SIM. So you are going to take your SIM out and let me take your phone with me. I will take it to New York and throw it off a ferry on the Hudson. This device is pretty sophisticated. If they are monitoring it, it will seem you have either jumped or fallen to your death."

"You would do that for me?"

"Of course. After that, if you need my services again, you will have to pay. I consider my debt to your father cleared."

"You got a deal."

There was a ping from the computer and he began to type furiously, muttering about how they had taken the precaution of covering their tracks. But after ten minutes he smiled. "OK, as you might expect, they are actually very close. They are on the outskirts of Salida, just past Poncha Springs, on County Road 220." He turned the computer so I could see it. I made a mental note, but he went back to his computer. "Let's see if we can get some satellite imagery."

He typed some more and spoke without looking at me. "You got a laptop with you?"

"Yeah."

"Tell me your email." I told him and he typed as I spoke. "OK, I have sent you a dozen pictures. It's the best I can do. It's not perfect, but it should help you some."

I frowned at him. I was wondering what he owed my father. "Thanks..."

"Don't mention it."

He disconnected my phone, opened it and removed the SIM card, which he handed to me. "You'll have to buy a new phone, but it's a small price for getting these bastards off your back. They are very dangerous, but I guess you know that already."

I smiled. "Yeah. They know that about me now, too."

He gave something that might have been a smile and said, "Don't tell me. Not now. Maybe some other time, I hope." He held out his hand. "Good luck, Mr. Walker."

We shook. "Good luck, Mr. Gantrie."

He climbed out and walked quickly back toward the airport.

I cruised down to South Tejon Street, where there was a computer store, and bought a printer, then I drove back up to Turret. I was keen to have a good look at the satellite images Gantrie had sent me. Knowing he was no longer in debt to my father made me feel better about accepting his help.

When I got back, Blueberry was sitting on the porch. I took the car around back, set it to recharge and walked through the bar to join her. On the way, I dumped the printer on a table and picked up a couple of cold beers and a chair. I handed her one and sat next to her, to look out over the empty dirt road.

She accepted the bottle and took a pull. "I'm going to sue you for destroying my business."

I winced but she didn't see me because she was looking at the empty road. Then I shrugged. "You probably made more out of me in the past couple of days than you made out of all your customers in the last month."

She turned to look at me. "You're going to pay?"

I frowned. "Of course. I always pay. Ask Maddox."

She turned away again. "I would, only, you know, he's dead, along with all his crew."

"I'll make it up to you."

She smiled, but not at me. "Yeah? How?"

"I'll find a way." After a while I said, "You like running a bar?"

She nodded. "Yeah. I'm good at it."

"OK."

She put her hand on my knee. "You get sorted?"

"Yeah. I bought a printer. I need to print some photographs."

She studied my face a moment. "What of?"

I smiled. "A ranch."

"Another one?" She looked worried.

"This one is different. There are no crazy crops to be burnt. No factories. Just a friend to rescue and a score to settle."

She shook her head. "You are the craziest son of a bitch I ever met. Can I help in any way?"

"Yeah. Stay safe."

I got up and went inside to start unpacking the printer. She followed and sat watching me in silence. When I had hooked it up to my laptop and installed the drivers, I downloaded the emails Gantrie had sent me and started printing the satellite images. It was a slow process.

I drained my beer and held up the bottle. "You want another?"

She looked up at me and seemed to study my face. "What are you going to do when you've rescued your friend and settled your score?"

I shrugged. "I don't know. I guess I'll go back to Wyoming, keep fixing cars."

She smiled, but it was a sad smile. "Wouldn't you like to fix cars in Colorado?"

"I think the sheriff of Chattee county might have something to say about that."

"I guess he might."

She stood and went to look at the photographs as they spewed out of the printer. She looked at one and then another, frowning. "I know this ranch. It's out by Poncha Springs, on the 220."

"How come you know it?"

"I had a Saturday job there when I was sixteen. In the stables, cleaning the horses, sweeping out the manure. That kind of stuff."

"Who does it belong to?"

"I never met the owner. It was a big ranch. I never went near the house. I did see them a couple of times, though. They didn't look like local folk. They looked more like they were from out east. He was always dressed in a suit. She was always in a fancy dress. I don't think they ever set foot in the stable. Foreman didn't like 'em much. Said they had no business running a ranch."

"Could it have been the man who got out of the Audi today?"

She shook her head. "No. That type. But he was older, and bigger. He had long hair over his collar, brushed back. But I only saw him a couple of times, getting in and out of his car. He had a foreign car. British. A Rolls Royce or a Bentley or something like that." She paused, studying my face. "What are you going to do to them?"

I shook my head. "If he has nothing to do with taking my friend, I won't do anything to him. But if he is involved, I'll kill him."

She stood and walked to the bar. "How can you *say* that? Like it doesn't mean anything? Like it's going down to the store for a bag of potatoes? It's a life, Lacklan! A human life!"

I stared at her, wanting to agree with her, but I couldn't.

"Because without killers like me, good people like you and my friend would be at the mercy of people like them."

She looked like she was close to tears. "Is that true, Lacklan, or is that your excuse? How close are you right now to becoming people like them?"

"Close," I said, "But I haven't lost my humanity yet. Not yet."

"Leave it, Lacklan. Leave it and walk away. I don't know what your story is, but I can imagine. I know you're a good man at heart. Walk away from it, go back to Wyoming if you have to, but stop while you are still human."

I stood and went to her and cupped her face in my hands. "They will torture her, and eventually kill her. If it was you, Blueberry, trapped on the inside, I wouldn't let them do that to you, either. It's who I am."

"You wouldn't?"

I shook my head. "Will you help me? Will you go over the photos with me and tell me everything you know about it."

She nodded and placed her hands on my chest. "OK." She hesitated a moment. "When you've done the job, will I see you again?"

I nodded and smiled.

"Try and stop me."

But we both knew it was a lie.

Seventeen

IT WAS A HALF-HOUR drive from Turret to Salida on roads with no traffic. I left as the sun was setting, along county roads 184 and 175. They were no more than broad dirt tracks winding their way through deep, remote gorges, all the way down from the mountains into the valley. I came out just north of Smeltertown, to the west of Salida, in what looked and felt like a vast, dry riverbed with a railway line running through it. I crossed the railway at a level crossing, drove up a dirt track and found myself in downtown Salida, on the curiously named F Street.

A right on East 3rd took me to Poncha Boulevard, among low, flat buildings, acres of residential areas bathed in listless amber street lights, and stars and stripes hanging limp in the sultry evening air; a dispirited testament to a time when America was the land of the brave and the free.

The streets were practically empty. The people of Salida were not standing by their flags. They were indoors, making outraged posts on Facebook and Twitter about what they'd seen on TV, that America was no longer the land of the free.

What had Tau said? The pills, in combination with social media...

I turned left onto Poncha Boulevard. It was long and straight, with parkland and scattered houses on either side of the road, set among large sweeps of gardens. Plain trees obscured the street lamps, casting dappled light on the blacktop and the sidewalks; sidewalks that were mainly beaten earth or raw concrete. Pretty soon I left Salida behind me and I was among broad, flat fields that were lost in the darkness, with just the occasional glimmer of light from a farm building or a cottage here and there.

After three or four miles, I came at last to Poncha Springs, which is little more than a scattering of houses and shops. I turned right on Main Street and felt the hot burn of adrenaline in my gut. A mile down the road was my turn. A mile down the road I would start exacting retribution.

I moved, silent and fast, out of Poncha Springs, and within moments, I found the dirt track on my right that led into the ranch. I turned onto it and killed the lights, then rolled noiselessly into the blackness. I followed the track for half a mile, past a cluster of shacks and barns and turned left into some woodlands that bordered the fields. There I killed the engine.

From the trunk I pulled my now depleted kit bag. I set up the bow and removed six of the aluminum arrows. I thought about the Smith & Wesson cannon, but decided against it. What I needed tonight was deadly silence.

I fitted the night-goggles and set off at a run through the woods toward the paddocks that surrounded the house. My breathing and my thudding feet crunching on the fallen leaves sounded loud in my own ears. After a couple of minutes, I came to the edge of the tree line and dropped on my belly. The house was about three hundred yards away. It was a large, three-story, colonial building, with a porch at the front and a broad terrace on the first floor, over the porch. There were lights in most of the windows and I could see a guy with an automatic weapon standing by the front door.

I knew there would be more walking the grounds. They might believe that I was in New York, jumping into the Hudson, but after what I had done to them the night before, they wouldn't be taking any chances.

I scanned the area and slowly they began to emerge, strange black silhouettes against the green background glow.

The nearest was two hundred yards away, a hundred paces from the house, patrolling with what looked like an assault rifle slung over his shoulder. A second had his beat at right angles to the first, along the north side of the house. I figured there must be another at the back and a fourth on the south side. The remainder would be in the house.

The house itself was floodlit, but where the guards were patrolling was outside the pool of light, in darkness.

I ran fifty paces toward the north wall, at the side of the house, hunched over and in silence, then dropped and crawled on my belly. I lay waiting, watching the guard walk closer. He stopped maybe thirty yards away and lit a cigarette. The smoke looked a ghostly green through my goggles. He hailed his pal, then turned and started walking away at a slow stroll. I crawled after him as his colleague withdrew. When he was twenty or twenty-five paces away, I got on one knee, nocked the arrow and drew. The bow was orange osage, very hard and very springy, with a draw weight of sixty-five pounds, the perfect balance between power and accuracy. The arrows were broad heads and razor sharp, designed to enter easily and cause maximum bleeding. One of these could kill an ox in a matter of seconds.

I lined him up and loosed. There was the softest whisper. He seemed to hesitate for a second, then sat down and gently lay on his side. Now I had to act fast, while the guy at the front was walking away from me. I sprinted toward the back of the house, nocking and drawing a second arrow as I did so. I came to the corner just as the guard emerged. It was a long shot in the dark, maybe a hundred and twenty yards, but I am a good shot and I had no choice, I had to take it. I didn't aim. It was an intuitive shot. I drew back to my ear and let the barb fly.

He paused, like he thought he'd heard something. Then started in surprise as the arrow thudded home into his heart. He looked down at the feathers for a moment as he bled out internally and, like his pal, he just lay down to die.

I had seen from the satellite photographs that there was a large chestnut tree on the far side of the house that had branches that reached out as far as the first floor terrace. I ran now, with total disregard for noise, nocking a third arrow and drawing it half way as I went. If my timing was right, the next guard would be on his return walk. Keeping outside the glow of the floodlights, I spotted him on his way back. This shot was easier, only fifty or sixty yards. I pulled back to my ear, took aim and loosed. Another whisper and he went down like his colleagues.

I had been scanning the walls for CCTV cameras. I hadn't seen any. I figured, like Blueberry had said, most of the time the place was run as a ranch and the valuable stuff was in the barns, protected by an alarm system. The plan to hold Marni here had been improvised, like the security. I was pretty sure if there was a CCTV camera, it was recording and not being monitored.

I made sure the guard at the front was at the far end of his patrol and sprinted for the tree. I leapt, scrambled up, and pulled myself in among the branches. There was one that spread out and would take me to the edge of the terrace, about six feet above it. But by the time it got there, it was real thin and I wasn't sure it would hold my weight. It would be a gamble.

I sprawled out and began to snake along the branch. I didn't have a lot of time. Pretty soon the one remaining guard on the outer perimeter was going to notice that his two pals were missing. As I approached the terrace, the branch began to dip. I slid a little father and it began to give under me. I was a couple of feet away. I gave myself a heave, slid off and it sprang back behind me. My fingers seized at the balustrade and I scrambled with my feet against the wall, hauling myself up and over.

I had no time to waste. I stood and drew a fourth arrow. I fitted it to the bow and pulled. I found the guard at the front. He was standing at the far north end of his patrol, staring down, like he was looking for his colleague. He didn't have to look long. I sent him where his friends were waiting for him, with a barb that went in through his left clavicle and sliced through his lungs. He died quickly and silently.

I removed my goggles and lay on the terrace. The lighting below was the bright glare of floodlights, to avoid people approaching the house unseen. Up here, on the terrace, it was a more tenuous light, probably meant for dining, or having drinks. Some of it came from a couple of wrought iron lamps attached to the white walls, and some from the large, plate glass doors.

I took a few seconds to look around. The floor was tiled in terracotta, dotted with plant pots and flower pots. It was about twenty-five feet across and twenty feet deep. At the far end a whitewashed wall rose in steps toward the red, slated roof, where a smaller terrace gave way to a French door under a couple of gables.

At the center of the lower terrace, where I was, a wooden table with six chairs stood with a brass oil lamp sitting on it. I crawled over and lay peering through the chair legs at the big, plate glass doors.

Inside I could see a brightly lit drawing room. It was opulently furnished, more for show than comfort. There was a large, marble fireplace that stood cold, and in front of it a sofa and two armchairs. Tau was sitting on one of the chairs. Another man was standing by the fire, holding what looked like a martini. From Blueberry's description, I guessed he was the owner of the ranch. He was big, probably six-two, with a barrel chest and a great mane of hair swept back from a big forehead. He was wearing a tweed jacket with a green waistcoat and I could make out the gold chain of a fob watch. The way he was talking, you could tell he was a pompous ass.

I could only see the back of the sofa, but I could make out the top of a head just above it.

A plan is something you make before you start an operation, not during. One thing they drum into you day in and day out in the Regiment is you plan your operation meticulously and in detail before you go in, so that every eventuality is covered. That way you don't fuck up. And if you do fuck up, you know what to do about it.

But you can only plan if you have advance information. When you have no information, you have to make it up as you go along. Now I had to decide what to do next. For a moment, I regretted not bringing the Smith & Wesson. It would be simple to blow away the plate glass, shoot their knees out and make them tell me where Marni was. But I had no idea how many men were in the house, and a plan as crude as that could go ass over tit very quickly.

I saw the big guy laugh. Tau laughed too, though it seemed to hurt his face, which was still bandaged. A door opened and a manservant and a couple of maids came in carrying a table-cloth and a tray of cutlery.

The manservant stopped to speak to the big guy. I couldn't hear what they were saying, but their body language suggested they were talking about eating on the terrace. They seemed to think it was a good idea because Tau and the third person stood, picking up their glasses as they did so. The third person was a woman. She turned to move toward the terrace, and I saw her face.

It was Marni.

Eighteen

I DIDN'T HAVE TIME to be surprised or think about what it meant. I had five, maybe ten seconds to move before they came out and found me. I pulled my cell from my pocket, pressed record and slipped it behind a plant pot. Then I sprinted, leapt and sprang up the stepped wall and onto the upper terrace. There I positioned myself in the shadows where I could see the table, but I knew I could not be seen.

I heard the glass door slide open and voices came up to me on the warm evening air. It didn't sound like a cruel interrogation. It sounded like old friends having a chat.

Tau was saying, "I don't mind telling you, it was nice to have a couple of weeks off. I'd been in New York several times over the last year..." They were making their way across the terrace while the maids laid the table and the manservant brought out a trolley with a tray of decanters and glasses. Tau was leaning against the balustrade, still talking. "But it could have been Miami, San Francisco or Singapore. You know what I mean? Boardrooms look the same the world over."

The big guy and Marni laughed. "I hear you, Tau. But it gets easier as you get older. They rely more on your wisdom and less on your energy. I do most of my work from my office here, now. Or in Washington."

"Where are you based in Washington, Rho?"

139

"Chain Bridge Road, equidistant between Palisades and Wesley Heights." Tau nodded approval. Rho smiled at Marni. "Are you familiar with the area, Marni?"

There was a smile in her voice. "Not yet. But I plan to become familiar."

They all laughed and Rho patted her shoulder. "That's the spirit. Shall we sit?"

The maids had finished and had withdrawn. Rho sat at the head of the table. Marni had her back to me and Tau was sitting across from her. He looked in surprisingly good shape, and I could only imagine that he had managed to shield himself behind one of the Jeeps when the car exploded. Next time he wouldn't be so lucky. But even as I said it to myself, I had a sick pit in my belly and I could feel my hands shaking. What the hell was Marni doing?

The manservant had taken a bottle from an ice bucket and was pouring white wine into their glasses. Rho raised his and proposed a toast.

"To good friends, allies, and a successful future."

Marni chinked her glass against theirs and said, "Here's to that, and wealth – lots of it."

They laughed. Tau said, "That will come. It should not be your primary focus, though. Think mainly of your function in the overall plan. You are part of the family now. We will look after you. Believe me, more wealth will come your way than you can possibly imagine."

"Sounds good to me."

The maids came out with a bowl of oysters on a bed of ice. Marni helped herself and after a moment said, "Tau, have you any more news about Lacklan?"

I felt a hot twist in my gut.

Tau shook his head. "I'm afraid not. Shortly after twelve, he seems to have driven to Colorado Springs and taken a flight to New York. There he seems to have taken a ferry at the World Financial Center. We have no idea where he was going, but that's where his signal stopped abruptly."

"He could simply have thrown his phone in the river."

Tau nodded. "We have people making inquiries on the ground. But witnesses saw somebody jump in."

She was quiet for a moment. They watched her. Rho asked suddenly, "Will you miss him?"

She shrugged. "I had barely seen him for ten years. What's to miss?"

I felt a hot flush of anger, and suddenly a mad hatred welled up like a poison in my veins. I raged against believing what I was hearing. But betrayal was not new to me. Ultimately, it was what I expected, from everybody. I nocked an arrow. I could finish them right now, in a matter of a few seconds. But I knew that wouldn't be enough. I had a madness growing inside me. I wanted Omega. I wanted to bring the whole damned thing down, and my father and Marni with it.

She was talking again, picking an oyster from the bowl.

"We are going to talk shop now."

Rho laughed. "I expected no less of you."

"Edward has made it clear that the Earth can't sustain more than nine or ten billion people. I have gone over his figures with him and I agree. Now, nine billion people is not going to make life easier on the planet, even for an elite. It is going to make the world an ugly, difficult place to live in. Explain how you are going to make this work to our advantage."

Rho leaned back, holding his glass like Yorick's skull. "You refer to Wilson? Edward Wilson?" She nodded. He nodded back. "A clever man. Fortunately, nobody listens to him." He sighed, like he was gathering lots of interesting thoughts together. "You have to put it all into the context of the overall plan. These seven, almost eight billion people, who are expanding exponentially, are at present consumers..."

She raised a hand. "Most of them are too poor to consume in any significant way."

He chuckled. "But you see, those countries where poverty is at that level invariably spend a fortune on weapons. Weapons are one of our five biggest sources of revenue."

I saw her nod slowly. "OK, but they are still breeding and they are still expanding, and they are spilling over into the West as refugees."

Tau laughed. "Now, now, Marni, don't let the Thought Police catch you saying things like that!"

She swallowed another oyster and took a sip of wine. "Understand me. If I am joining up with Omega, it is because I want to live in a world that is nice to live in. I am not into some Soylent Green shit dystopian future."

"And neither are we." It was Rho. "Quite the contrary. Like you, our aim is to create what our founders called the New Atlantis. A place, as you so succinctly put it, that is nice to live in. Nice by *our* standards. Not by Seth or Billy Joe's standards, who would be content with a TV and a fast food burger joint."

Tau was nodding. "We take that as read."

Marni spread her hands. "So what do we do with these nine billion people?"

Rho raised one fat finger. "First, we use them to create wealth. They help us to do this by providing us with cheap labor and by buying our weapons. So while we are generating wealth we are preparing. Now," he raised a second finger. "You may have noticed the happy synchronicity that brings us global warming at the same time as this explosion in population."

"How is that happy?"

Tau wagged a finger at her. "You need to shake off those mental chains, Marni. They are all very well for high school ethics one oh one, but if you aim to climb up the evolutionary scale, you need to change your thinking."

"I do? OK. Tell me."

"Within the next few years, it is impossible to be precise, the temperatures around the equator will start to rise dramatically..."

"I know. That has been my point all along. That is why I am sitting at this table..."

Rho raised a hand. "Bear with me. Both your father and you highlighted this point. I know. Now, what you also said, and what we could never have you publish, was that as temperatures rise, the regions to the north and south of the equator will begin to experience drought on a scale never before seen. Famine will follow drought, punctuated by flooding and hurricanes. In short, gradually, the areas between parallel forty-eight north and forty-eight south will become practically uninhabitable, and certainly non-productive in terms of food. And this of course will lead to mass migration north."

He sat back and sipped his wine. "In nature, in ancient history, climate change has always lead to mass migration. Of course today, with this human plague sapping the planet, we call it a refugee crisis instead. But it's the same thing."

Marni sighed. "I don't mean to be rude, Rho, but so far you are just quoting my own research at me."

He smiled. "Where your research has fallen short, Marni, is exactly where Tau pointed out. Your moral limitations. You assume—you take it as a given—that we must help these refugees, these billions of starving people. But once we have prepared, created the infrastructure of the New Atlantis, their purpose will be served and we will not need them anymore."

Marni flopped back in her chair. "Wow..."

The maids came out again and removed the dirty dishes and the bowl. The manservant poured the red wine and the girls brought out three dishes of roasted duck breast. Rho waited for them to withdraw and started cutting into the tender breast.

"You see," he said, "since the middle of last century, we have been creating the conditions, as dear Margaret used to say, creating the conditions for violent social unrest. You have no doubt been aware of the rising popularity of far right parties, and a general feeling amongst a growing portion of western society of grievance against stupid and incompetent governments and politicians, who do not seem to have the best interests of their people at heart; politicians who force mass migration and rampant Islam upon a helpless populace. The lines are drawn, the seeds are sown, for a violent backlash."

Marni sounded shocked. "And that's a good thing? How?"

"My dear Marni, you have been complaining about the exorbitant growth in population. I am now offering you drought, hurricanes, tsunamis and war as means to thin out that population."

"But these are things you cannot control..."

"That used to be true. And this was the purpose of the research that Professor Weitz was conducting in Turret, until your friend Lacklan came along. My God, that man is destructive. I tell you, Marni, that man had a very troubled soul."

"I believe you are right."

"The point is, natural disaster, and war, will account for a good many people. But civil conflict within Europe and the USA will reduce the population drastically and also have the added bonus of creating a new mood of unity and solidarity. That is a base on which we can build."

"So your plan," said Marni, "is to select a population..."

"It is already selected, naturally, the western population. Those people who have been bred on social media, computers, TV, who have practically no critical faculties left at all. They are ripe for exploitation."

Tau spoke up. "It would take a minimal intervention, using the sun beetle, to create a population happy to serve, happy to create a New Atlantis on a reborn world."

She shook her head. "That is a pretty crazy vision."

Rho shrugged and spluttered. "In 1917, a vision of a world with eight billion inhabitants, where you could talk instantly to anyone anywhere on the planet, and see them on a hand-held screen, where it was against the law to smoke in public and the air was poisonous to breathe, would seem like a nightmare fantasy. Yet it is a reality. These violent changes are *inevitable*, Marni. What we aim to do is manipulate them, ride them, so that at the end, we are on top, and the people who survive are submissive and compliant."

"What about Russia, China, Europe...?"

Rho raised both hands palm out and smiled. "You have hardly touched your food. I think that is quite enough shop talk for tonight. You need to assimilate this new vision, and begin to fall in love with it."

She spread her hands. "You're right. Just let me ask you one thing. Did any of the bugs survive? Or did the fire wipe them all out?"

They were silent for a moment. Then Tau said, "We are checking, but we are confident some have survived. If not, we go back to the drawing board to recreate them."

I closed my eyes. My head was spinning. For a moment I didn't know what I was doing there, what my purpose was. I had come here to rescue her, to help her, but she didn't want to be rescued. She was one of them, and my death meant nothing to her. So, if she didn't want to be rescued, why the hell had she put that picture on the board? Why had she left her diary for me?

What was her game?

Nineteen

THEN I HAD A FLASH of clarity. I knew what to do, but before I could act there was a shout from out in the darkness and the sound of running feet—a lot of running feet. The guards had been found. I stood and drew my bow, targeting Tau, determined that this time he would not survive. But even as I did it, he and Rho stood and four armed men burst onto the terrace, shouting to them to get inside.

Three of them took up positions looking down into the grounds. The fourth, a big, dark guy with a long black ponytail, addressed Rho.

"The boys on the perimeter! They are all dead, sir, shot with arrows. We checked all the rooms in the house. He ain't inside. He's still out there."

That was the last mistake he ever made in his life. One and a half seconds later, he was looking down at his chest, wondering why he had a feathered shaft sticking out of it, as his consciousness and his life ebbed away.

It is a fact that people take a full four seconds to react to unexpected violence. If the violence is completely silent, it takes a little longer. The three guards were still staring out into the blackness of the night. Rho was frowning at his lieutenant as he slowly sat down in the chair he had been occupying. Tau was looking about him with a 'What the...?' expression on his face.

Only Marni reacted. She got to her feet and said, "No..."

All of that happened in a single second. By that time I had nocked my second arrow, pulled and loosed. It whispered on the night air and thudded home into the farthest guard's heart, protruding two inches from his chest.

I had time to pull my Sig and take out a third guard before Rho started screaming, "*He's here! He's here! On the roof, you assholes! Here on the roof!*"

I tried to get a bead on him, but he rushed at Marni, grabbed her with his left arm and dragged her in front of him. Meanwhile, with his right he pulled a gun from under his arm and let off two wild shots in my general direction. Marni was thrashing and kicking, clawing at his hand. Tau had clambered over the table and was scrambling for the door, screaming, "*Up here! Up here!*"

The remaining guard had seen me and let off three rounds, nicely grouped. I ducked and they hit the wall behind me, whining and singing off into the darkness. He paused a second and I put a single shot through his forehead that sent him backward over the balustrade.

Now we had a stand-off. Rho had his arm around Marni's throat and his gun to her head.

"All right, Lacklan, give it up. It's over. You have come this far for her, we both know you are not going to let any harm come to her. Drop your weapons and come down here."

I laughed. "I've been here since you strolled out with your martinis. I heard your whole damn conversation. You think I give a rat's ass whether you shoot her? If you don't, I will."

I knew as I said it I had overplayed my hand. He smiled. "So go ahead. At this range, if you put a bullet through her throat, you'll kill me too. So do it. I know you have the skill. What's stopping you?"

I took careful aim. He was right and I had the wild rage of betrayal inside me. I felt like my brain was on fire and I was sick to my stomach. My father's betrayal I had learnt to live with, and my mother's indifference. But this, from Marni... Part of me wanted to punish her, to make her pay, but I couldn't pull the trigger.

Instead I said, "You're bluffing. You need her alive."

Tau came running back onto the terrace with eight guards, all holding assault rifles. They took up positions, training their weapons on me. I didn't stand a chance in hell.

"Do I?" Rho said. "Maybe I already have from her everything I need."

"If you had, Rho, you wouldn't be feeding her oysters and telling her she's part of the family."

He shrugged. "You're not wrong. But don't be over-confident, Lacklan. That is just the easiest route to what we want. There are other ways." He turned to Tau. "What do you say, Tau? Shall we discreetly withdraw and leave the boys to play with Marni for an hour or two?" He looked up at me. "Are you a voyeur, Lacklan? Would you enjoy that? Or perhaps that is too subtle." His face was suddenly twisted with hatred and cruelty. "Maybe it would be quicker to remove her foot with a blunt knife!"

Then he was screaming with rage, "*Come on! Tau! Grab her!*" and he and Tau were wrestling her toward the table while three of the guards swept the plates and the glasses onto the floor, where they shattered into shards. Marni was thrashing and screaming. They had her on her back, gripping her arms and legs. Rho had her ankle and he was shouting, "*You! Get me that knife from the floor! Quick!*"

I stood. "Stop."

He turned to look up at me. His face was flushed with rage. He continued screaming, hysterical, "*I should do it anyway! You cunt! I should fucking do it anyway you piece of shit! You fucking cunt-shit!*"

I raised the Sig and aimed it straight at his eye. "Go ahead."

Tau put his hand on Rho's arm. "We have him. Don't blow it." To me he said, "Get down here."

"Let her up."

Rho straightened his jacket and smoothed his hair. Marni got to her feet. She stared at Rho a moment and made a grab for the knife he had been about to use on her ankle. Tau raised a hand. "Ah-ah! Let's all just de-escalate this situation. We do this right and nobody gets killed tonight. Am I right, Rho?"

Rho smiled at her. "I am sorry, Marni. It was nothing personal. We do what we have to do."

She whirled round and stared up at me. Her eyes were bright with anger and frustration. "You should *not* have come!"

I felt a bitter twist of anger in my gut. "Yeah, I can see that now. I'm sorry I interfered with your business arrangements. My father thought you were in trouble. Looks like he's as much a schmuck as I am."

I climbed down the wall and threw my weapon on the floor. One of the guards picked it up. Rho stepped over to me. I could see his intention in every step and every twitch. I gave him the dead eye and spoke very quietly.

"I haven't much left to lose, Rho. I don't much care if I die here tonight. So you better think carefully about what you do next. Touch me and I'll break your fucking neck."

I meant it, and he knew it. He hesitated a moment and snapped, "Tie him up. Put him down in the cellar."

Four of them grabbed me and pulled my arms behind my back. I felt a plastic zip-tie bite into my wrists. I was watching Rho's face, trying to figure him out. "What do you want with me? I see why Marni could be useful to you, but what do you want with me? Why not just kill me and be done with it?"

He stepped over real close so his face was only an inch from mine. "You have all the questions, Lacklan, and I have all the answers. That is the way it is going to stay, but you can be sure, the moment I have no more use for you, you'll die."

Marni was still staring at me. Two of the guards held her arms. She looked mad. "How did you *find* me? They said you'd gone to New York!"

"I guess I'm not the only one with questions."

Rho turned to his goons. "Tie her up too. Put her in the boiler room."

She turned on him. "What? Wait! No! Why? This doesn't change anything? Why are you doing this?"

Tau laughed. "Oh, my dear, it changes everything."

I smiled at her. It wasn't a nice smile. "Congratulations on your new friends, Marni."

They dragged me away and I heard her scream after me, "You *idiot!*"

They took me down the stairs and into the kitchen. There they unlocked a door and pushed me down a flight of concrete steps into a large cellar. There were racks of wine against the walls and a long, wooden table with glasses and decanters on it and other paraphernalia, as well as a shelf stocked with wheels of cheese and bottles of mineral water. They sat me on one of the chairs and zip-tied my arms and ankles to the back and legs.

One of them, a big redneck with pale blue eyes, patted my face and grinned. "Don't go drinking the wine."

They made to leave. "Hey."

He turned back to look at me.

I said, "I'm going to kill you first."

He laughed and they tramped up the stairs.

Like I said, planning is everything. It was clear to me when Rho put his gun to Marni's head that either I was going to be shot or I was going to be tied up and imprisoned. So I took what precautions I could. Always be prepared for a fuck-up.

I wriggled my right wrist and my Zippo dropped into my palm. This was going to hurt, but pain is something you can get over. Death isn't. I flipped the lid and thumbed the flint, then angled the flame onto the zip-ties. The pain on my wrist was excruciating, and the smell of singed flesh was sickening. But after a couple of seconds the bonds snapped. I bent forward and burned through the ones on my ankles too.

I stood and stretched and thought about breaking out of the cellar. But I decided against it. I needed to think. I needed to understand what the hell Tau and Rho wanted with me, why they had suddenly turned on Marni as soon as I appeared; and what the hell Marni was playing at.

I went to the wine racks and selected a Cotes du Rhone, Famille Perrin Reserve from 2012. A wine like that should breathe for at least an hour before drinking, so I poured from a great height to get the air into it, pulled a pack of Camels from my pocket and lit one, and set about choosing a good goat's cheese. Then I sat and ate and drank and smoked.

And thought.

Twenty

MORNING CAME WITH THE sound of the key in the lock at the top of the stairs. Then several pairs of feet tramping down. It was the redneck with three of his pals. He stood staring at me and pulled his piece from his waistband. I was sitting at the table, having a breakfast of cheese and red wine.

"You're a fuckin' piece of work, Mister." He turned to the apes behind him. "Would you take a look at that? Tie him up again."

He covered me while three of them approached me. I finished my cheese and stood. I put my hands behind my back and turned away from them. They fitted another zip-tie and shoved me toward the stairs.

They led me up through the kitchen back to the drawing room on the first floor. Tau was seated in one of the armchairs and Rho was standing, leaning on the fireplace again, sipping coffee. The glass doors were open onto the terrace and outside I could hear birds getting busy about the morning.

Rho said, "Sit down, Lacklan. We need to talk."

I sat on the sofa and smiled at him. "We do?"

"I think you are intelligent enough to understand that nothing we do is motivated by personal feelings."

I turned my smile on Tau. "That makes me feel a lot better. I thought after you had me strung up and beaten to within an inch of my life, you didn't like me. That really hurt, Tau."

Tau crossed his legs and lit a cigarette with a match. As he shook out the flame he spoke around the butt. "Try not to be facetious, Lacklan. What Rho is driving at is that everything you heard us say to Marni last night was genuine. Our intention was—and may still be—to initiate her into Omega."

"Where is she?"

Rho asked me, "Do you still care for her?"

"I don't give a rat's ass about her."

His smile told me he knew I was lying. "Our purpose is to find the quickest, easiest way of recovering Professor Gilbert's research, and Marni's research. If that means inducting her into Omega, so be it."

Tau took over. "But we have a feeling that, even if we do induct her, we may never get hold of that research. Marni could well—and understandably—hold on to that research as an insurance policy."

He said it like he was being very reasonable, and I ought to appreciate that. I shrugged. "So?"

He laughed tolerantly, like an amiable uncle guiding his nephew towards intelligent thought. "So, when you showed up, alive and well instead of dead and bedraggled in the Hudson River, we realized immediately that we had a much more elegant way of getting to the research. We had options."

I began to realize why Marni had called me an idiot. "You think I know where the research is?"

Tau squinted at me through the smoke from his cigarette. "Let me be clear with you, Lacklan. Once a body is inducted into Omega, that person's safety is sacrosanct. As long as they remain loyal to us, we remain loyal to them. Only—and I mean this literally—*only* betrayal is punishable."

I yawned as rudely as I could. "You want to get to the point, boys?"

Rho scowled. "Give us that research and we will induct you into Omega."

"Fuck you."

"We have other options, Lacklan."

Tau cut in. "Think about it before answering. We could use a man like you. We could use your skills. You *have* impressed us. If you can give us Dr. Gilbert's research, and Marni's, your place is guaranteed.."

"Fuck you."

They looked at each other and shrugged. Rho turned to the redneck and said, "Jim, bring her in."

He left with a couple of his goons and Tau turned to me. "One of you knows, or perhaps both of you know, what Marni has done with this research. You can understand that if it got into our enemies' hands, research such as that could be very damaging to us."

"Who are your enemies?"

He spread his hands like I was being absurd. "Think! China, Russia, Saudi... even Europe. There are even groups at home who are a little squeamish about our plans." He laughed. "So we are not short of enemies, Lacklan!"

Rho went to refill his cup from a coffee pot on the coffee table. "Not one of them comes close to being a threat right now. We have vast resources at our disposal. But even so, it does not do to be complacent. We want that research, Lacklan, and we will do whatever we need to do to get it."

Tau shrugged. "One of you knows. Maybe both of you. The answer is simple. We will torture one of you, probably her..."

He glanced at Rho, who shrugged, then nodded. "...until one of you talks. It's not original, but it is effective."

Rho spoke in a loud voice. "It will be grotesque and irreversible. You should know that."

There was a noise outside and Marni was shoved in. She looked pale and scared. I said, "You're wasting your time and you'll spoil the rugs. I don't know where it is. If you kill her, you'll lose your only chance of finding it."

"Are you suggesting we should torture you?"

I shrugged. "You think it will make any difference? She doesn't give a damn about anyone but herself. Torture me as much as you like. I can't tell you anything and she won't tell you anything. Your best plan is to go back to where you were at last night."

Rho chuckled. It was a comfortable, uncleish sound. "You are either naïve or stupid, Lacklan. You are certain that Marni has no feelings for you, but I am far from convinced. We shall find out when we remove your eyes with a soup spoon, shan't we?"

I raised an eyebrow at Marni. "If you have any surprises up your sleeve, now would be the time."

She averted her eyes. "I'm sorry, Lacklan. Whatever you think, this is not easy for me either."

"Stop, you're breaking my heart."

Outside I heard the distant thud of a chopper approaching. Rho smiled. "Speaking of surprises..."

Tau stepped onto the terrace and looked up at the sky, shading his eyes. The sound got louder and soon his hair and his jacket were flapping in the downdraft from the rotors. He turned and nodded to Rho with an upturned thumb. Rho spoke over the noise of the landing helicopter. "It seems you have a visitor to witness the proceedings."

I listened to the dying whine of the turbines as it settled outside. I knew what it meant and I looked Marni in the eye. "Tell me you haven't bought into this shit, Marni. Tell me it's not true."

He face flushed and she screamed at me. "*For fuck's sake, quit whining! Get real, Lacklan! All your fucking life you've been chasing unicorns and rainbows. Life is not like that!*" She pointed at Rho. "This! *This* is reality! *This* is what counts! Money, power. The rest of it is *bullshit!* Do you understand me?"

Tau was standing in the terrace doorway, watching her with interest.

I shook my head. "You are wrong."

She sneered, "Where the fuck have you been living for the past ten years? Cloud Cuckoo Land? Don't you ever *read?*" She pointed at me. "You need to get a grip on reality, Lacklan. You are a loser and you are about to pay the price for it. I *told* you in London. But you won't get it into your thick, loser skull. It is *over* between us! Why the *fuck* did you come here? If you think I am going to come to your rescue now, think again, pal!"

I spat the words at her. "I told you why I came after you. Because my father asked me to. He's an even bigger schmuck than I am."

Rho raised his hands. "Lacklan, your father is anything but a schmuck. If you had a fraction of that man's intelligence, you would have saved us all a great deal of suffering, and you would probably have a seat on the Council by now. Sadly, you are everything that Marni has said you are." He moved away from the fireplace and opened the drawing room door. His face lit up. "Gamma, Bob, come in. You have arrived, as always, at just the right time."

My father and my brother stepped in. They stood, like echoes of each other across time, both looking down on me, both shaking their heads.

"There is one thing, Lacklan, that I can always rely on you for," said my father, while Bob smiled. "I can always rely on you to fuck up."

"You set me up, you son of a bitch."

He moved to the armchair and sat down. Bob pulled over a chair and sat next to him, watching me, gloating.

"I needed her found. I knew you'd find her, and I knew you would lead us right to her. You never could do anything right, could you?" He turned to Marni. "I told them to offer you a place."

Her voice was angry, almost shrill. "Which I accepted! And everything was going fine until this *clown* showed up! Will you *please* tell them that I intend to cooperate!"

He sighed and shook his head. "It is a little late for that, Marni. You have to give us the research. It's the only way we can trust you. Otherwise," and he and Bob leered like ghastly reflections of each other, "we start cutting bits off Lacklan."

Twenty One

TAU WALKED INTO THE room from the terrace door and said to Jim, the redneck, "Go get a plastic sheet."

I felt a jolt of something close to panic. Jim dispatched one of his boys and came toward me. He put my neck in an arm lock and dragged me onto the floor. Three of his boys assisted him by cutting the zip-tie behind my back and gripping my arms. I heard my father's voice, mild and agreeable.

"Well, Marni, what do you say? Shall we go for the left hand, or the right? We are doing this for you, so you get to choose."

"I don't give a damn what hand you go to work on. I am not giving you the only insurance policy I have. I am willing to do a deal, but I am not willing to put myself completely in your power, Robert. Surely you understand that?"

I heard him sigh, and at the same time I heard the rustle of plastic as the goon came back into the room. They kept talking as though nothing special was happening on the floor in front of them. "Haven't I always looked after you, Marni? Have I ever let any harm come to you?"

I shouted, "This son of a bitch killed your father!"

Jim wrenched on my neck and yanked me up. They spread the sheet under me and then slammed me down on it. I felt Jim's knee press into my back. He said, "Which hand, boss?"

My father sighed again. "The left. Have you got the pliers? Are they blunt? This really has to hurt a lot. OK?"

"You got it, Boss."

I tried to struggle, but strong hands had my legs. Somebody twisted my right arm into a half Nelson behind my back, and somebody I couldn't see pulled my left arm out in front of me. My heart was pounding and I could hardly breathe with Jim's choke hold on my throat. My father said, "Make him watch."

Jim forced my head around. I looked at Marni. Her eyes were wide and I could see her hands trembling in her lap. My father was smiling at her. Bob was grinning at me. There was a fat, sweating goon hunkered down next to me holding a pair of pliers. He said, "What finger, Boss?"

My father said, "What finger, Marni?"

Her voice was taut. "Look, I've told you! It makes no difference to me. I don't *care!* I am willing to deal with you, Robert! Why are you doing this?"

He gave a small laugh. "The pinkie, Tony. Nice and slow."

Robert, my brother, got down on his knees to help force my fist open, and Tony slipped my small finger into the pliers. He gripped the handles and began to squeeze. I felt the iron blades bite, not on the knuckle, but on the bone. I knew that if they did this I would be out for the count.

I screamed, "*All right! She can't tell you because she doesn't know!*"

My father said, "Stop." Tony and Bob looked disappointed. My father was frowning at me. "What?"

I spoke frantically, in desperate bursts. "She doesn't know where the research is. She gave it to me the night of the fire! We had an arrangement! I would dispose of it in a way that would insure her safety. But I wouldn't tell her where or how! For *exactly* this reason. So nobody could force it out of her!"

He sat back in his chair with a fat, complacent smile on his face and she screamed at me, with tears in her eyes, "*I thought you'd taken it to New York! They told me you'd gone to New York! Why the fuck did you come back?*"

"*Shut the fuck up, Marni!*"

My father spoke quietly, silencing both of us. "That is so typical of you, Lacklan. It is just you, through and through. Always wanting to be the hero, always wanting to be Sir Galahad. And always fucking it up at the last moment. It was a good plan. Why couldn't you have seen it through?"

Rho interrupted. "So where is it, Lacklan?"

I struggled. They held me hard. "I need some kind of deal. I need some kind of assurance."

My father snapped, "Take off his finger!"

Tony squeezed. I shouted, "*Wait! For fuck's sake! I'll tell you!*"

Tau spoke. "One more line of bullshit, Lacklan, and I will personally remove not one, but all five of the fingers on your left hand. Are we clear?"

"Yes!"

"So where is it?"

"It's up in Turret. On the slopes of Green Mountain. Near the cabin where you found Marni."

Marni gasped. "*What?* How fucking stupid are you, Lacklan? *Jesus!* I could have done that myself! I didn't fucking need you to do that!"

"I came to save you, you ungrateful bitch! Only to find out you didn't *fucking need saving! Because you'd become one of them!*"

Rho and Tau were looking at my father, who was studying my face. He said, "It actually has the ring of truth." To me he said, "Can you draw us a map?"

"No. I need to show you." I saw Tau narrow his eyes. "Come on! There must be several million fucking pine trees there! You could spend years digging under each one and never find it!"

My father nodded. "Put Marni in the cellar. Take Lacklan back to Turret." He turned to me. "One stupid move, Lacklan. Just one. A simple phone call and Marni dies. And I assure you, it will not be a swift, painless death. The boys will have their fun. That is the way it is."

I looked him in the face. "I am telling you the truth. But you have to give me some guarantee, some insurance. And get these fucking apes to let go of me." He gave Jim a nod and they got off me. I got on my feet and looked at him. "Well?"

"If you haven't lied, if you hand over the research to us without complications, I will use my influence to protect you. But the games have to stop now, Lacklan, and I do mean *now*." He turned to Jim. "Take the chopper and three of the boys. Check in every hour. I expect you back before nightfall." He looked back at me. "If I don't hear from Jim..." He checked his watch. "At twelve-thirty, then at one-thirty, then..."

"Yeah, I know what every hour means."

"Marni will die. Be smart for once in your life, Lacklan."

"I understood it the first time you explained it." I looked at Jim, right in his pale blue eyes. "Let's go."

We went down the stairs and across a huge hall decorated in mock Rococo and Grecian columns and Roman statues. They even had a small fountain in the middle of the floor. As we stepped through the main door and out into the morning sun, my mind was racing. I could hear my first sergeant in the Regiment, a giant Kiwi with hands like bricks and a voice like a rasp. "*Always* have a plan. *Always!* The right plan is more deadly than any gun or any knife. Got it?"

Got it, Martin. So what was my damned plan now? My plan was, make it up as you go along.

We climbed on board the chopper. Jim sat up front and told the pilot where we were going. I was sat in the middle at the back, between Tony and a black guy the size of a small building. He had a pencil moustache and a really tiny amount of beard on the end of his chin. He slammed the door closed and the rotors started their slow, thudding spin overhead. Next thing, the turbines were screaming and we were lifting up amid a whirlwind of downdraft. Then we were away, skimming over treetops and fields, toward the foothills of the mountains.

We flew for fifteen minutes without speaking. The noise of the rotors made talk impossible, but as we drew in over Turret, the pilot shouted to Jim, "Where do you want me to put it down?"

Jim looked back at me. I leaned forward and shouted in the pilot's ear, "There's an esplanade, with a fork in the road, about one mile past Turret, just before Green Mountain! You can put her down there!"

He nodded and as I sat back I let the cheese knife slip into my cupped hand. I turned to the huge lunk on my left and said, a bit too quietly to be heard, "So what's your name?"

He frowned at me, "Huh?"

"Shit for Brains? They called you that?"

He scowled. "What you sayin'?"

I leaned forward and shouted, *"I said what's your name?"* and as I shouted I rammed the cheese knife home into his heart. He went into spasm. I heard Tony shouting, *"Hey! What you doin'?"*

I wrenched the knife from Shit for Brains' chest and turned back to Tony, shouting, *"I don't know! Something happened!"* and slammed the knife back-handed into his solar plexus, tearing the diaphragm and making it impossible for him to inhale or exhale. As he tore at his throat and his eyes began to bulge, I pulled the knife out and plunged it between his vertebrae, at the base of his skull. It had all happened in a matter of seconds. Jim was frowning in the mirror. I released Shit for Brains' safety belt, opened the door and shoved him out. Then Jim started bouncing and screaming.

"What the fuck! What the fuck!"

I reached over to Tony, took his automatic from under his arm and stuck it in the back of Jim's neck. I shouted again.

"Call Gamma. Tell him cell phones have no reception up here. Tell him everything is going according to plan and you will call him from the landline in the diner at Turret in two hours. I told you I would kill you first, Jim. You got lucky. I need you alive right now. But irritate me just a little, and I will throw you out of the chopper, alive. Do we have an understanding?"

I could see in the mirror that he was very pale. He nodded. "Yes."

"Do it now. Put it on speaker."

He dialed and I heard it ring twice. My father's voice said, "What?"

"Yeah, Mr. Gamma, um, our cell phones ain't gonna have no reception up here. But everything is going just fine, so I was thinking, I'll call you from the landline at the diner in about two hours. That OK?"

There was a protracted silence. Then he said, "Let me talk to the pilot."

I rested the muzzle of Tony's pistol against the back of the pilot's neck. He spoke calmly.

"Yes, Gamma. I'm here."

"Is everything under control?"

"Everything is A-OK, Sir."

Jim took the phone back. "Is that all right then, Gamma, sir?"

"Two hours precisely."

"Yes sir."

He hung up and looked at my reflection in the mirror. I smiled at him and leaned close to his ear to shout, "*You know what, Jim?*" He watched me, scared. I went on, "*I don't need you anymore.*"

I shot down, through his right clavicle, so the bullet ruptured his heart, but there was no risk of damaging the chopper. I looked in the mirror. The pilot was watching me. It was hard to tell what his expression was. I said, "Put it down on the road."

"Are you going to kill me?"

"Not if you don't make me."

Maybe he believed me. I wasn't sure whether I believed my-self. Either way, he took it down in a deep gorge and set it on the dirt road amid a great cloud of dust. I said, "Leave it idling and get out."

He did as I told him and stood by the side of the road. I got out on my side and walked around to face him. "Are you armed?"

He shook his head.

"You called my father Gamma. Why?"

"That's his title in the Omega organization."

"So you're a member of Omega?"

He shrugged. "Not really. I'm employed by them as a pilot."

I pointed toward Turret. "Half a mile that way you'll find a phone. If I ever see you again, and you are working for Omega, I'll kill you. Get another job."

He nodded, turned and started walking. I climbed in the chopper and took off, turning it back toward Salida, my father and Marni.

Twenty Two

I CAME IN LOW AND SET the chopper down on the far side of the woods where I had left the Zombie the day before. I jumped out and ran, dodging through the trees, ignoring the pain that still lingered in my ribs from the beating I'd received at the farm, until I came to my car. I yanked open the trunk and pulled out my now practically empty kit bag. From it, I took the Smith & Wesson 500 cannon. Something told me I was going to need it. I slung the field glasses around my neck and set off at a jog toward the ranch.

I stopped at the tree-line to observe the house. I could see one guy on the porch, smoking. He had an assault rifle. On the terrace above the porch I could see my father, Tau and Rho sitting at the table. I glanced at my watch. It was twelve-thirty. They were probably about to have lunch. There was another guard with them, standing at the far corner. He also had an assault rifle. I paused for a moment to think. There could not be that many guards left. Doing a quick mental recount I figured there could not be more than five or six. And the remaining three or four had to be on the inside. One at least would be guarding the entrance to the cellar, where they had Marni. The other two would be in the drawing room and on the stairs. That's where I would put them.

The night before I had noticed a building not far from the back of the house. I now saw it was a garage. It was open and there was a guy in shirtsleeves washing a black Porsche 911 just outside the entrance. Beyond it I could see a Bentley and a Buick Regal. I crouch-ran through the trees till I came up behind the building. Then I sprinted the few yards to the garage and flattened myself against the wall. I couldn't use Tony's automatic because it had no silencer. It would have to be a manual job. I pulled my fighting knife from my boot and slipped up to the corner. He had his back to me and was polishing the glass in the windows.

There is something unpleasant about stabbing a guy—any guy—in the back. There is something ugly and unfair about it. Fortunately, I am not sentimental. I took two noiseless strides, clamped my left hand over his nose and mouth and rammed the razor-sharp blade into the side of his neck, slicing outward as it went through. He bled out in a couple of seconds, spraying blood over the car, then sagged to the ground. He'd made a mess of the window. That would have to be cleaned again.

I felt in his pockets for the car keys, wiped my knife on his pants and sprinted to the kitchen door. I didn't pause. At this stage there was nothing to be gained from caution. I opened the door and stepped in. My calculation was right. There was one guy sitting at the kitchen table reading the *National Enquirer*. He had a mug of coffee and he was smoking a cigarette. The manservant who had tended the table the night before was at the cooker, making lunch.

I didn't break step. I threw the knife and it thudded home through the cook's fourth and fifth intercostals to the left of his spine. He wheezed and quivered. The guy reading the tabloid looked up in astonishment as the chef collapsed. By then I was behind him. He tried to get to his feet, but my arm was around his neck. I squeezed hard, lifted and twisted. When I felt his vertebrae crack I let him drop back into his chair and pulled my knife from the manservant's back.

I unlocked the cellar door and slipped down the concrete stairs. Marni was tied to the same chair where they had put me. She saw the knife in my hand and looked at my face. She was scared. I put my finger to my lips and walked behind her.

"Lacklan, you have to listen to me..."

"Shut up."

She hissed in a whisper. "No, listen to me. You were not supposed to come here. This was not the plan."

I cut the zip-ties from her wrists and her ankles.

"Whose plan?"

She stood. "That does not concern you."

I grabbed her shoulders and turned her savagely to face me. "When I am laying my life on the line, killing people, it concerns me!"

"You don't understand. You *can't* understand!"

"I understand that I have been used! And I understand it feels a hell of a lot like I have been betrayed!"

"You know that's not true!"

"Do I?"

"Lacklan..."

"What was that talk on the terrace last night? What was the fucking talk in the drawing room this morning?"

"It's too complicated."

"*Whose plan?*"

She hesitated. "Mine..."

"What is your plan?"

"I can't..."

I shook her and spat the words at her. "*Listen to me! I will not be used and then thrown aside! I should cut your damn throat right where you stand for what you have done to me!*"

"Lacklan!"

"*What the fuck is going on?*"

"I..."

"If you want me to trust you, you had better come clean with me, or I swear, if you have used and betrayed me, I will bring bloody hell raining down on you, Marni..."

There were tears in her eyes. "No, Lacklan... I would never do that. But there is no time... no time to explain now."

I put the keys to the Porsche in her hand and said, "It's parked outside the garage. Go. Contact me when you're safe. But, Marni, you had better have a damn good explanation for what I have seen and heard since last night."

She nodded. "I thought you trusted me..."

"So did I."

I moved toward the stairs. Her voice stopped me.

"Lacklan..."

I turned. "What?"

"Is it true? Is it true that he killed my father?"

I nodded. "That's what he told me. He was ordered to by Omega, because of the research he was doing. The research that cost him his life, and which you now want to trade for money and power."

There was a spasm of anger behind the tears in her eyes.

"You have to know that isn't true, Lacklan."

"All I know is what I have heard and what I have seen. If that is wrong, then show me something different." We stared at each other for a long moment. When I realized she wasn't going to speak, I gave a laugh. It sounded harsh and bitter in my ears. "This is the last time I play the schmuck for you, Marni." I turned back toward the stairs. "Now go! I'll keep them busy while you get away."

I ran up the stairs. She followed. In the kitchen she grabbed me and stared into my face, like she was trying to communicate telepathically with me. I shoved her out the back door and closed it in her face.

I slipped into the hall, moved quickly to the bottom of the stairs and peered through the banisters. The guy was sitting there staring at his cell phone and smiling.

I made it to the fourth step before he looked up. At that distance it was an easy throw. The long, broad blade severed his windpipe and his vocal cords, so the only sound he could make was a slight, bubbling hiss. I took hold of the handle and sliced sideways. It was a strange place to die, sitting on a chair on a landing half way up the stairs.

That left three. One was on the porch and he was my first priority, because any minute now Marni was going to go roaring past in the Porsche. He had an assault rifle and he could riddle the car with bullets in seconds.

I was across the hall in three strides. I ripped open the door and lunged at him. His reflexes were good. He dodged the knife and tried to bring the rifle around. I couldn't let him fire. That would alert the remaining guards. I grabbed the barrel and in the same movement I slashed up through the tendons in his wrist. He gasped and goggled at the half-amputated stump. Before he could scream I smashed my elbow into his jaw and rammed the knife into his solar plexus. As he suffocated I eased him to the floor and put him out of his misery by severing the spinal cord in his neck.

Now that left two. One directly above me on the terrace, and the other I figured was in the drawing room. I fancied the odds. The time for fighting in the shadows was over. I pulled the Smith & Wesson from my belt and stormed up the stairs.

He obviously assumed it was one of his pals coming up, because I found him standing in the doorway, frowning. His weapon was hanging behind him. When he saw who it was charging toward him, he gaped and reached for the rifle. He was too slow. I braced myself, aimed in the general direction of his thorax, and pulled the trigger. The noise was deafening. An S&W 500 will punch a hole clean through a two-inch steel girder. It punched a hole the size of a tennis ball in his chest, tore out the back of his rib cage, and threw him ten feet into the room.

I ran. I could see my father staring at me with absolutely no expression. Tau, Bob and Rho were goggling. The last remaining guard was running around the table toward me. He couldn't shoot yet, because the spray of bullets might hit his bosses. That was too bad for him. I lined him up and blew his neck from his shoulders. His head spun six feet into the air before dropping and rolling toward the balustrade. It bumped against a potted palm before his body folded and fell.

I turned to the three men sitting around the table. The fourth, my brother, was on his feet, retching over the side of the terrace. My father was looking at his hands and shaking his head. Rho and Tau were staring at me, their eyes wide with terror. I was wondering why I hadn't heard the Porsche yet.

"I have three rounds left," I said, "Let's talk about what I do with them."

Twenty Three

I PULLED OUT A CHAIR with my foot and sat on it. I kept
them covered with the Smith & Wesson and with my left hand
I pulled a pack of Camels from my pocket. I fished one out and
lit it. I inhaled all the way down and let the smoke out slow.

My father still hadn't looked at me. He spoke to his hands.

"What have you done, Lacklan?"

"I have been killing. It has been a very busy morning."

My father grunted. Tau stood, like he was going to do
something, but just stared at me, and then at my father. Rho
buried his face in his hands and Bob turned back to the table,
leaning on the back of a chair. "You..." he pointed at the body.
"You decapitated..."

My father interrupted him. "Jim?"

"He's dead. So are Ape Man and Tony."

Tau blurted out, "What about the pilot?"

I looked him in the eye and lied. "Dead."

"Where's the chopper?"

I smiled. "Why don't you have a walk around the house,
Tau? You'll see them all. They are all dead. Each and every one
of them. Even the guy you had cleaning your Porsche."

My father looked worried and raised his eyes from his
hands to try and read my face. "What about Marni?"

I laughed. "What do you think, *Dad*? You still think I'm a
loser? You still think everything I do winds up being a fucking

disaster? You want to depopulate the fucking planet. I'm doing my part." I looked up at Tau. He was trembling. I snarled, "Sit down before you piss your pants, Tau."

He sat. Bob sat too, like he didn't want to be left out and ignored. "What do you want, Lacklan?"

I laughed again. "You guys. You lurch..." I looked at each of them in turn. Rho still had his head in his hands. My father was still watching me, trying to read me, and Tau still looked like he was going to burst into tears. My brother was pale gray and his mouth was sagging open. "...You lurch from sneering and blustering about your power and your wealth, to falling on your knees, begging, offering your riches in exchange for pity; in exchange for your worthless, parasitical lives. You think of yourselves as lords of the Earth, but you have no idea what power really is."

My father looked impatient. "What have you done with Marni?"

Maybe she had taken off across the fields on foot. There was no sign of the Porsche. I stuck the cigarette in my mouth and leaned forward. I pulled back the hammer on the Smith & Wesson and pointed it at Tau's head. "You know what power is, Tau?"

He was sweating and his teeth were starting to chatter. "No, please don't. Just say what you want..."

"Power is not money and power is not influence. Power is the ability to inflict violence. And the more violence you are capable of inflicting, the more power you have." I swung the gun round and aimed it at my father. He didn't flinch. "What do you say, *Daddy*, am I right? That is the lesson you have been teaching me since the day I was born. Violence is the source of power. Violence, and above all, the willingness to use it. Isn't that right, *Pop*?"

"I am going to ask you one more time, Lacklan. What have you done with Marni?"

I ignored him and turned the cannon on Rho. "Ability to inflict violence, and willingness to inflict violence. I guess that makes me the most powerful man at this table." I turned to meet my father's gaze. I narrowed my eyes and shook my head. "You're like kids, with your names from the Greek alphabet and your Marvel Comic experiments in mind control. But there's not a fucking man among you." I paused, then said in a flat voice, "I killed her."

He closed his eyes and went pale. "No, Lacklan..."

I narrowed my eyes. "What did you think? That you could use me like some sap? That you could get me to do your dirty work for you, find the girl, and then you and she and Bob could wander off into the sunset to become fucking billionaires together, while you all laugh at how fucking stupid I am?"

He opened his eyes again and tears spilled onto his cheeks. "You have no idea what you have done."

"Wrong again, old man. I know exactly what I have done. But I am just wondering what it is I need to do to make *you* wake up to the fact that I know *exactly* what I am doing."

I stood suddenly and stepped behind Rho. With sickening violence, I grabbed his hair in my fist and slammed his face down onto the table. He cried out and I rammed the barrel of the cannon onto the back of his neck. I pulled back the hammer with a loud click.

Tau was on his feet squealing, "No!" My brother covered his face with his hands.

Rho was sobbing. My father looked away. "Please son, sit down. We understand what you are capable of."

I was staring at Bob. "What's the matter, Bobby? You were happy to see my fingers cut off, but you can't bear to see this guy's head blown in?" I turned to my father, Gamma. "How many people," I asked him, "do I have to kill to make you listen to me?"

"I am listening. Please, sit down and stop this. What do you want?"

Rho was still whimpering, "God, please, don't kill me. Please don't kill me."

I said, "I want in."

Tau glanced at my father. He kept swallowing. "We can do that, right? That is *not* a problem."

"Shut up, Tau. I know my Greek alphabet. You're the rookie at this table. My brother is nothing." I pointed the revolver at Rho. "The guy pissing his knickers here is a middle manager." I looked at my father. "But above you, old man, there are only Beta and Alpha. So if anybody is going to make it happen, it's you. Right, *Dad*?"

He nodded. "I can make it happen."

"Who is Alpha?"

He shook his head. "You don't know him. He is not a public figure."

"What's his name?"

"Kill me if you want to. I will not tell you."

I stood. "Rockefeller, Rothschild, Gates..."

He smiled without humor. "No, no one so obvious. I will arrange for you to meet them."

"Them?"

"Alpha, Beta, Delta and Epsilon. We are the five, the cabal. I will arrange a meeting. Now please, let us stop this. What have you done with Marni's research?"

"I mailed it from Colorado Springs to an attorney in New York with instructions to put it into a safety deposit box in a bank. You can guess the rest."

He sighed. "What attorney? What bank?"

"Fuck you."

"How do I know...?"

"Seriously? *Seriously?*"

He held up his hands. "All right."

But it was too late. Suddenly, I'd had too much. Too much stupidity, too much madness, too much cruelty, too much of these gutless parasites who believed they were entitled to piss on the world and be thanked for it. Above all, too much betrayal. I looked at my brother. In my mind I could see him gloating, holding my hand open so that Tony could take off my finger. I screamed, "*Seriously?*"

And then I was on my feet, driven by a force that terrified even me. I walked behind Tau and he cringed away. But I wasn't after him. I went past him and grabbed Bob by his hair. My father was crying out, "Lacklan, no! Wait!" But the rage was stronger than I was. I dragged him to the balustrade, grabbed the seat of his Armani pants and tipped him over. There was a brief, twisted shout and a sickening thud.

Tau and Rho were transfixed, goggling at me. My father was staring, with soaking cheeks, at the empty space over the balustrade where, a second earlier, his eldest and favorite son had been. I spoke very quietly.

"You want to ask me again how you can be sure I am telling the truth?"

He shook his head. "Please stop now, Lacklan."

"What happens to this mind control operation now?"

"It depends..." He was still weeping silently, staring at the balustrade.

"On what?"

"On whether any of the sun beetles survived." He stood slowly and went to look over the side at the broken form of his son. His face seemed to fold in on itself. "Bob..."

I felt a twist of pain and grief in my gut. But I choked it off and said, "You get me in. I want Kappa or above. You understand me? And I want control of that program. Or I'll bring down such hell on you that the last twenty four hours will look like a picnic with the girl scouts. Am I clear?"

He nodded. "Yes."

He sat back down in his chair, covered his face and started to sob like a child. Tau and Rho looked uncomfortable. I returned to my chair and fished out a cigarette, wondering what the hell I was going to do next. That was when things started to go seriously wrong. It started when I heard Marni's voice, speaking from the sliding doors to the terrace. She said, "You killed my father, Robert. And you have to pay for that."

Twenty Four

I TURNED TO LOOK AT her. She was holding a Glock she must have picked up from one of the corpses.

"Marni, what the hell are you doing?"

My father had lifted his tear-stained face from his folded arms and was frowning at her, uncomprehending. "You are alive..."

"Yes, I'm alive. Why? Did you send a couple of your boys to kill me?"

He shook his head, still frowning, "No...of course not..."

"But you killed my father."

He turned to me. "You shouldn't have told her."

"Why wouldn't I?"

He smiled. It was an odd, sad smile. "To save her the pain...?"

My voice was a rasp. "You could have done that, but not killing him."

Now he laughed, a dry, empty laugh. "You talk of killing! Look around you, at your handiwork."

"I would not kill my best friend on the orders of a *fucking* organization!"

"But you would kill your own brother out of vengeance!"

I shook my head, "No, Robert, he may have been your son, but he was no brother of mine."

He gestured at me and flopped back in his chair. "This! This is why I never inducted you. This is why I favored Bob. You have no clarity. You are like your mother. All passion and no brain."

Marni stepped closer and raised her gun in both her hands, aiming at his head. She was ice cold, and at that distance she could not miss. She spoke like an automaton.

"But look where it has got you both. He is the one holding a gun, and you have accrued the hatred of everybody that matters to you." She narrowed her eyes. "How? What kind of tortured, twisted emotional contortionism did you have to go through, to justify to yourself the murder of your best friend; the father of a small girl who adored him? How could you live with yourself?"

He looked down at his open palms, as though he might still find blood there. "You think it was easy for me?"

She gave a small laugh, as though she was astonished. "You want me to feel sorry for you?"

"No." He shook his head. "I just wish I could explain, and that you both would understand. I had no choice."

She was incredulous. "No *choice*? No *choice*?" She repeated it, like the second time would have more meaning. "No choice but to murder your best friend?"

"He understood. He entrusted your care to me."

She shook her head. "Enough. I won't listen to anymore of your twisted, tortured madness."

He closed his eyes, accepting the inevitable shot that was to come. I shouted "*No! Marni! No!*"

I leapt forward and struck the barrel of the gun up. It detonated and the shot went high over his head. She turned a face of pure rage on me and swung at me with the pistol. I blocked the blow with my forearm and grabbed hold of her shoulders, shaking her and shouting, "*Marni! Snap out of it!*"

Then something that felt like a brick smashed into the back of my head. For a moment I blacked out and fell to the floor. It must only have been a couple of seconds, but it was enough for Tau to scramble across the drawing room and clatter down the stairs, with Rho close on his heels. I opened my eyes and saw my father standing, stooping, looking down at me. A couple of inches away Marni came into focus, lying on the floor, groping savagely for the pistol she had dropped. I looked my father in the eye and snarled, "*Go!*"

He turned and hurried, old and bent, toward the stairwell. Marni's fingers closed on the automatic and she raised it to fire. I shouted, "*Marni! Stop!*" and lunged at her. She fired but again the shot went wide. She screamed.

"*What are you doing? Let me get at him! I have the right!*"

As she screamed she thrashed, clawed at me and smashed the butt of the gun in my face. Then she was up and running, too. My head was reeling and splitting with pain. I struggled to my feet. As I stood, I saw my phone behind the plant pot where I had left it the night before. I recovered it and ran for the tree. I vaulted over the balustrade, grabbed the branch and swung down. Then I sprinted for the garage. I was too late.

Tau was running cross-country toward the woodlands. I knew where he was going. He had figured that that was where I had put down the chopper. Rho was clambering into the Buick and my father was close behind him, headed for the Bentley. Within seconds, the engines were roaring and they were kicking up gravel and dust, speeding down the driveway. As they passed, I saw Marni fumbling with the keys I'd given her, as she slammed the door of the 911. I took off at a fast sprint after Tau.

I made the distance to my Zombie in record time. My lungs felt like they were tearing apart, and my head had at least three invisible hatchets embedded in it. But none of that was important. What was vital, what was essential, was that I stop Marni from making a mistake that could have incalculable consequences for her, and for the world.

I swung the beast around and gunned the silent engine. Across the field, I could see the three cars moving onto the 202. Between me and them, there was a mile of dirt track. I promised myself that if I got out alive, I would replace the entire suspension. Then I hit the pedal. I flew over the potholes, the ruts and the rocks by sheer inertia, and covered the mile in less than a minute. But in that minute, they had put almost two miles between me and them. I skidded onto the blacktop doing sixty.

The Zombie will do naught to sixty in just over one and a half seconds. I floored the pedal and instantly sent one thousand eight-hundred foot-pounds of torque to the rear wheels. I saw the nose lift like a dragster and felt myself crushed into the seat as the needle rose in little more than a second from 60 to 170. In absolute silence. If they were doing 120 MPH, I was gaining on them at fifty.

In less than a minute I saw the distinctive black shape of the Porsche 911 looming up ahead and I eased up on the pedal. She was right up Rho's ass. The Buick was a nice car, but it was no match for the huge power and performance of the Porsche.

I didn't give a rat's ass about Rho, but I knew Marni and I knew she had never killed anybody. That was not her and when her rage and madness had passed, I knew she could not live with a man's death on her conscience. Not even a man like Rho.

But what was just as important was that I had understood why my father—Gamma—could not die; why it was essential that he should live.

I swerved and gunned the engine to overtake her, intending to place myself between the Porsche and the Bentley, but she pulled out, missing me by an inch and blocking the road. I hit the brakes and swerved right. She stayed ahead of me.

The road had been long and straight heading west out of Salida. Now, as we approached Maysville, the road turned sharp left. As we closed on the bend, Marni clipped the Buick's rear nearside fender. Its brakes screamed and it swerved. I floored the pedal and cut the corner, trying to get ahead of the Porsche. She hit the gas hard, heading me off to the side of the road. A loud blaring like an express train made me look ahead. A huge truck was bearing down on me at a combined speed of over 200 MPH. I braked hard and swerved, pulling in behind Marni and missing her by a couple of inches. The truck thundered by, still blaring its horn.

In the confusion, the powerful Bentley had surged ahead. Marni was harrying the Buick like a whole pack of wolves all over a wounded caribou. Every move he made, she was on top of him, and he had neither the speed nor the performance to get away from her. But I knew her real interest was my father, up ahead in the Bentley. And I could not let her get to him.

I floored the pedal again and tried to overtake. Again she swerved into my path, but now she drew level with the Buick.

I heard two cracks and his rear left window shattered. She was shooting at him.

Another left turn and we were climbing toward the mountains. The Buick rammed the side of Marni's Porsche, sending her skidding off the side of the road, raising clouds of dust behind her. I slowed, thinking she might give up and I could talk to her, but she hit the gas and took off after them again. I followed, nosing into her side, trying to place myself between her and my father. But once more she pulled alongside the Buick, and as he tried to side swipe her, she put three more rounds into the side of his car.

Another truck appeared around the bed in the road up ahead and came thundering for a head-on collision with the Porsche. I slowed to give her space to pull in. She slammed on the brakes. The Buick pulled ahead and she swerved right. The truck skimmed past.

I spun the wheel left and pulled alongside her, screaming through the window to pull over. She ignored me. She lined up right behind the Buick, a couple of inches from his fender. She was holding the Glock in her right hand and, leaning forward slightly, she rested the butt on the dash for stability. I hammered on the horn, screaming at her not to be stupid. But I saw the Glock kick four times, her windshield shattered, and I slammed on the brakes. Marni did the same as the Buick skidded and careened across the road, slamming into the bank and rolling over.

As I stared at it, at what she had done, she took off with a squeal of hot rubber after my father. I accelerated past her in a couple of seconds and placed myself between her and the Bentley, then started weaving and slowing, allowing him to pull ahead of us. I was trying to think where the road led, where he could go. We were in the middle of nowhere, climbing into the mountains. All I could think was that a hundred and sixty miles west, at Grand Junction, he could pick up the I-70, to Denver or Utah. It didn't seem like a hell of a plan, but as far as I could see, it was all he had.

He had managed to put a couple of hundred yards between us and Marni was going crazy behind me, weaving back and forth across the road and leaning on her horn. We sped through Monarch and then the road started to climb steeply and the bends became sharper. It dawned on me that on each hairpin, for a few second, she had a clear line of fire at the Bentley.

The road turned into a sharp bend ahead as it climbed. My father had taken the corner and was now accelerating up the hill across the gorge, only a hundred and fifty yards away. In my rear-view I saw Marni stop and get out. She took her time to go round the car and lean on the roof. She took careful aim. I started to reverse and as I did so she emptied her magazine, one shot after another in a steady hail of bullets. I stopped and stared at the Bentley. If she had missed, which at that range was very likely, he had got away.

For a moment, he climbed steadily. But then I saw him swerve, careen across the road and go over the edge. I turned and stared back at her. She climbed in the Porsche, turned and sped back the way we had come. I floored the pedal and covered the distance in a few seconds. I screamed to a halt where his car had gone over and stared down into the gorge. I could see it, wedged between two trees, with the hood buckled and a trail of smoke rising out of the engine. If he had survived, it would be a miracle.

I scrambled down, clutching at bushes and sliding on my ass as I went, wondering how the hell I was going to get him out of there if he was alive. Finally, I reached the trees where the car was wedged. The incline was steep, practically vertical, with the trees growing out at an almost horizontal angle.

The car was on its side, leaning against a giant pine, with the hood mashed up against another. I placed my feet on the rear wing and tested it for stability. It seemed to be firm. Then I inched along until I came to the passenger door. I crouched down, grabbed the handle and heaved. The door was heavy and the position I was in was awkward, but I managed to raise it and peer in.

The airbag had deployed, then deflated, and he was slumped against the side of the car, with blood oozing from a gash on his head. I lay on my belly and felt sick as I heard the car creak and felt it shift. I waited and let it settle, then leaned in and reached for his wrist. There was a pulse. It wasn't strong, but it was steady.

I sat up and looked up the slope. There was no way I was ever going to get him up there. I pulled out my cell and dialed 911.

Twenty Five

IT TOOK OVER THREE hours to extract him from the car and stabilize his condition enough to fly him by helicopter to the Penrose and St. Francis in Colorado Springs. Sheriff Mitch Hanafin made a brief appearance. He had looked at me, but hadn't questioned me or even spoken to me. He had talked to the paramedics and left.

Eventually, I asked them where they were going to take him. They told me and I had driven on ahead.

By the time he'd arrived, dusk had fallen and night was closing in. I had assumed that he would be declared dead on arrival. But he wasn't. He was in a coma, critical but stable, and going into surgery. I'd asked what the surgery was for, but was told only that a surgeon would speak to me as soon as he could.

I spent the next six hours drinking black water that pretended to be coffee and trying to get some rest on waiting room chairs with hard seats and steel arms. At one AM, a doctor in surgical gear with bags under his eyes found me at the dispenser, getting another polystyrene cup of not-coffee and asked if I was Lacklan Walker. I said I was.

He sighed and looked troubled, like he was being forced to deal with a problem he didn't believe was his.

"I am Dr. Fischer. Mr. Walker, the surgery we have just conducted on your father, was to remove a piece of a 9 mm bullet."

I frowned. "A piece of a bullet? Not the whole slug?"

He made a face like he thought I should provide an explanation. "It was lodged in his chest. It damaged his right lung, but fortunately it did not cause irreparable harm. We are required to report cases like this to the police, you understand."

I nodded. "What is the prognosis?"

He sighed again. "He is eighty years old. He is obviously a strong man and he is basically in good health. But major surgery at this age..."

He left the words hanging. I narrowed my eyes at him.

"Basically good health? He told me he had terminal cancer of the liver."

Dr. Fischer raised an eyebrow at me. "I'm afraid he has either been misinformed by his own doctor, or he has lied to you, Mr. Walker. Apart from the damage caused by what I assume was a ricochet, he was in good health for his age. I assume the police will be in touch. Meanwhile, he has been transferred to a room, if you'd care to stay with him."

I said I would and he had a nurse show me where it was.

The room was dark and quiet apart from the bleep of the heart monitor and the irregular rhythm of his slightly labored breathing. There was a reclining chair and I settled in it, aiming to sleep. Instead, I stared at the dead glow of the city in the black glass of the window and tried to make sense of everything that had happened over the last few days.

I didn't get very far. Eventually I fell into a stressful slumber marred by dreams that were too vivid and plagued with nightmares.

I awoke suddenly to see gray light outside the window. I glanced at my father and saw that his eyes were open. He was staring at the wall. I said, "Dad?" and his eyes shifted to look at me.

He gave something like a smile and said, "It's been a few years since you called me that."

"Don't get used to it. It slipped out. How are you feeling?"

"I've been better."

"You haven't got cancer."

"I know."

"Why did you say you had?"

"Because I thought it was the only way I could get you to talk to me."

I nodded and we sat in silence for a while. After a bit, he asked, "What happened to Marni?"

"I don't know. She emptied her magazine into your car, then turned around and drove back toward Salida. Dad, you have to explain to me what is going on."

He nodded. "This is probably the only chance we are going to get. For a few hours, we seem to have slipped through Omega's fingers. Pretty soon Ben will be here, and then they will start organizing everything..." His attention seemed to drift. "I am so tired of them organizing everything, Lacklan."

"Why are you betraying Omega?"

He grunted. "You want to be careful saying things like that, Lacklan. They have eyes and ears everywhere. But still, I don't think there is much they can do to me anymore. When they told me to kill Frank, it shook my faith. I had always believed in them. I believed that they were the only people who actually offered a solution to the catastrophe that was facing humanity. I believed that what they proposed, though it required ruthlessness, at least offered hope. A solution." He sighed and tears began to flow again, down his cheeks. "But when they told me to kill Frank, I began to understand that the solution they offered was no solution at all. It was just a different kind of catastrophe; a different kind of hell."

I frowned. "Why did you do it?"

"They don't like insubordination, Lacklan. They require total obedience. They gave me an option. Kill him, or they would take him out along with Silvia and Marni. And they also told me that my own wife and children were at risk. I explained it to Frank and he understood. He was a good friend and that made it a lot worse."

He turned to stare into my face. He wasn't sobbing, but the tears were flowing freely. "I am not a monster, Lacklan. I am not a good man and I have been a bad husband and a bad father, but I am not a monster. Killing Frank—having to kill Frank—having him ask me to care for his daughter..." He shook his head. "It twisted me. I thought I was going to go crazy. They promoted me. They gave me more power and more privileges. Your mother left me, you grew to hate me. I was in hell, Lacklan. And I had no way out, because I knew that if I tried, they would kill you and Marni."

He wiped his face with the sleeve of his pajamas.

"Then when Marni started following her father's research, and she went missing, I decided they had to be stopped, but I also saw an opportunity..."

"What is it about Frank and Marni's research that is so dangerous to Omega? Surely every climatologist in the world knows what is happening to the climate. And as far as population is concerned, there is Wilson and a host of others. What is so vital about Frank and Marni's research?"

He frowned. "You haven't read it?"

I sat forward. "I haven't got it, Dad. She never gave it to me. We were both bluffing, so one or both of us could get inside the organization and find out what the hell you were about, and how we could stop you."

He closed his eyes. "Then she must have it still..."

"I don't know. I gathered some evidence. Some of those golden bugs, some shipping manifests..."

He smiled at me. "I wish I'd had the wisdom to appreciate you, Lacklan. You're a good boy. A good man. You realize now that she was never going to join Omega..."

I nodded. "I got that. When I lied about having the research, she went along with it and it dawned on me then. She said things, about London, that were designed to make me understand... But I was so mad. Why didn't you tell me you were working against them?"

He shrugged. "I told you I wanted you to protect Marni. I couldn't tell you more. You hated me so much, frankly, I wasn't sure I could trust you. We have wasted so many years, Lacklan. And I have nobody to blame but myself." He sighed again. "How did you realize, anyway?"

"It dawned on me, you kept manipulating the situation so that either Marni or I could blackmail our way into Omega. You wanted us on the inside."

He nodded.

I looked down at my hands. "Dad, what was in the letter that Marni received, that made her leave like that?"

He shook his head. "I don't know. I can only guess it was from her father."

I frowned. "From Frank?"

"From his attorneys, to be sent on a particular date."

"So it contained the whereabouts of his research?"

"I imagine so."

We stared at each other for a long moment. "What do we do now, Dad?"

"Find the research. Read it. Understand it. Find Marni, Lacklan. Protect her."

He closed his eyes and his labored breath rasped once and stopped. The steady bleep of the monitor turned into a single, high-pitched tone that sounded in my mind like a scream. And then doctors and nurses were running in their green jump suits, snapping instructions to each other, trying to save what could not be saved. Trying to hold on to a man who was dead.

I went down into the dawn. I climbed into the Zombie and slipped silently into the traffic, accelerating away from my dead father, speeding, refusing to allow myself tears, refusing to allow myself feelings, not knowing even where I was going. Knowing only I had to find Marni and make her safe. Knowing I had to find the men who had done this. Knowing I would hunt them down even to judgment day, and I would destroy them.

NOTE FROM THE AUTHOR

IF YOU LIKED *DAWN OF THE HUNTER* then please consider taking a second out of your day and leaving your thoughts behind for others.

It takes a couple seconds, but seriously would mean a ton to me and help get the word out there about my books!

If you'd like to read the next adventure, you can do so now by visiting my website and ordering the next book in the series: www.blakebanner.com[1]

All the best,

Blake Banner

---

1.   http://www.blakebanner.com/

95462281R00119

Made in the USA
Lexington, KY
09 August 2018